Accidental Abduction

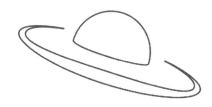

An Alien Abduction Book

Eve Langlais

Copyright and Disclaimer

Published by Eve Langlais
1606 Main Street, PO Box 151
Stittsville, Ontario, Canada, K2S1A3
http://www.EveLanglais.com

ISBN-13: 978-1461174523
ISBN-10: 146117452X

Chapter One

Maybe drowning won't be so bad. Megan's numb arms and legs agreed. Yet, despite the fact her whole body wanted her to stop moving—screamed it actually—she kept fluttering, moving her hands and feet just enough to keep her face above the waves. Every now and then she got a mouthful of salty water that made her choke and did nothing to cure her thirst. At least she didn't have to contend with the burning sun. Chances were she'd succumb to fatigue before the dawn arrived with its warming rays. Her sarcastic side—which was begging for a slap—piped in that she should also show thanks that she'd stopped shivering a while ago, her body acclimatizing itself to the Pacific waters she floated in.

Megan never intended to go for a swim when she set out for an evening cruise. She had her boyfriend—*stupid, freaking jerk*—to thank for her situation. And to think, she'd thought Cameron was "the one." He'd certainly said and done the right things in his wooing of her, and she'd enjoyed his company well enough, most of the time anyway, a rarity for her where men were concerned. She should have smelled something fishy when he'd immediately pushed for them to make everything joint soon after they moved in together—the whole cohabiting thing, again, his idea. His claimed, "Don't you trust me?" should have rung warning bells.

There was nothing as foolish as a woman in love, though, or, in her case, like. She'd fallen into the trap he laid, and not just the trap of a con man, but a death trap. *I wonder if my gravestone will say "Here lies Megan, screwed by a man, yet again."*

In her defense, no woman ever expected the man she loved—or liked—to betray them, even if, in her case, her track record with men should have provided a clue. She'd blithely agreed to go on a nocturnal jaunt with him, the moonlight cruise a celebration of sorts, the anniversary of their six month dating mark. A record for her. It would now also mark the date of her death. At least the bastard had toasted her with champagne before hip checking her off the boat with an exaggerated "oops." Then, he'd had the nerve to laugh when she'd asked him for help as she treaded water, incredulity not making her see the obvious at first.

It didn't take her long to clue in, and then she unleashed a litany of curses that would have made most seamen blush. Of course, the way she screamed in glaring detail the way she'd maim him when she got her hands on him might have factored in Cameron's decision to go through with his deadly plan—or precipitated it? She should have probably left off the gruesome details about how she'd emasculate him. But still, what other reaction did he expect given his action?

Megan heard his derisive laughter for a long time after he steered the yacht away in the dark with only the stars to guide him. Hours later—or so she assumed given the numerous scenarios she'd had time to run through her mind where she survived and got her revenge—she floated at the ends of her endurance and strength, fighting to live, even though she knew she had no hope of surviving.

A large wave rolled over her head, and she floundered under the water for a moment, almost giving up, too tired to care. Then she saw it.

A light!

Disbelief made her stare under the water at the bright beacon hovering just above her head. *Rescue?* She didn't question the improbability of it, just strained toward the brilliance using her last ounce of strength. Her head broke the surface of the ocean, and she blinked in the bright glare then blinked again as her body began to rise out of the water. *Did I die? Is this how my journey to heaven begins? Sopping wet and pissed?* Not to mention she'd always expected a much, *much* warmer reception when she finally did kick it. A poster child for pure living she wasn't.

A flopping fish lifted from the water in front of her and rose rapidly, slapping her in the face with its thrashing tail in passing.

What the hell?

Hell had nothing to do with it, though, she surmised. She peered around in slack-jawed disbelief as she and a football field of fish, along with other denizens of the ocean, rose out of the water, caught in some weird anti-gravitational field. And, no, she wasn't some kind of science geek for thinking that. She'd recently watched a marathon of *Star Trek* films because of Cameron, a true Star Trek fan. She'd never expected the inane fiction of the screen to ever relate to her life, but how else could explain why she and thousands of sea critters were floating as if weightless, drawn toward an illuminated maw whose edges she could barely make out?

It occurred to her to scream for help, but seriously, she wasn't an idiot even if she sucked in her choice of boyfriends. Besides, exactly whom did she expect to save her from an obvious alien extraction? In her current situation, abduction sure beat drowning any day.

Excitement replaced her exhaustion and resignation of her fate. She was about to meet extra-terrestrial life. Would they be green? Short or tall? Would they appear like a wrinkled E.T. or humanoid like her?

On top of these curious inner musings, doubt suddenly piled on. What if they were violent? Ate humans as a delicacy? Or—*gasp*—sold human females as sex slaves? Megan looked down at her plump frame, and her lips twisted ruefully. *I'm more likely to end up someone's main course than a sex slave.* While she didn't mind her plentiful curves, they didn't appeal to everyone, although she'd had more than one boyfriend claim it wasn't her body that turned them off, but her mouth. She didn't believe in keeping her opinions and criticisms to herself.

The slow aerial ascent took forever it seemed to reach the gaping hole in the bottom of the craft and about time, too, because, out of the water, she shivered with cold, her damp sundress clinging to her. She hugged her arms around her body, but it didn't help her chattering teeth.

What are the chances I'll be greeted with a towel? Looking around at the wide-eyed fish with their mouths gaping open and then shut soundlessly, she didn't count on it.

The bright light she'd mistaken for Heaven's doorway didn't diminish until she and her fellow aquatic abductees went past the lip of the ship. Then she goggled in astonishment because ringing the area on all sides were huge vats filled with liquid, oversized fish tanks if she wasn't mistaken—and not all of them from Earth. A purplish fluid in one certainly didn't resemble anything she'd ever seen and displayed the occasional black tentacle. Cool, although she wouldn't plan on going for a swim with whatever resided inside.

As the beam she found herself caught in angled up over the lip of an open vat, she noted something disturbing. All the other tanks were sealed shut. Her mind quickly came to an unwelcome conclusion. If she allowed herself to get dropped into the approaching aquarium, she'd find herself right back in the same spot, drowning.

"Not again," she muttered. She twisted herself to look around and noted a network of beams holding narrow walkways running above and around the vats. She needed to get onto one of those. Using her arms and legs, she kicked and pulled, much like she would if she were in water, if water were a thick molasses that fought her every inch of the way. Sweat beaded on her brow as she struggled against the beam's inertia, her progress slow, slower than the tractor beams implacable movement.

She brushed against other captives, their wet, slimy skin icky against hers, their lidless eyes watching her passage—*and I swear they're praying I don't make it.* Revenge for her regular Friday night sushi she'd bet. She almost didn't make it in time, the plopping sound of tumbling fish hitting water taunting her before her fingers grasped a cold edge of metal. She wrapped her hands tight around the beam and heaved herself over, cursing the fact she owned a gym membership she never used. Muscles straining, she brought her legs up to wrap around the metal support, the sudden loss of the anti-gravitational field's support making her almost fall as she suddenly held her full weight. Her aching muscles screamed in protest, but she held on for dear life.

The raining plop of objects hitting water made her turn her head to watch as the fish and other sea populations caught in the tractor beam were deposited in the huge tank. As soon as the last one hit the liquid surface, the beam shut off, and she blinked her eyes at the sudden loss of light. She could still see, albeit not as clearly, as dim circular lights surrounding the chamber provided only faint illumination. Dim vision didn't prevent her from hearing the whirring sound of machinery and the soft snick of the aquarium sealing shut, followed by a larger thunk, which she assumed meant the bottom portal had also closed.

Then it was silent except for a distant hum and her panting breath. Her arms trembled with the strain of holding herself, and it occurred to her that her first order of business should involve getting her feet onto firm ground.

Exhaustion brought her close to the point of hysteria at her inadvertent pun, and she giggled. Okay, maybe not firm ground but at least a surface she could stand upright on. Hanging like a monkey, she looked around and saw a walkway not far away, if she could only make her way over to it.

"Just like monkey bars," she reminded herself as she swung her body toward the next strut. Her hands caught the beam, and she let her legs go so her body could follow. She hadn't counted on the fatigue in her arms or how heavy her body would drag. Not to mention, she'd assumed a lack of or lesser gravity in space.

Wrong!

Her hands slipped from the beam, and she plummeted, her short scream of fright cut off as she landed in an ungraceful heap on something unforgivingly hard and blacked out.

Chapter Two

Tren, his feet propped on his main console, cursed as an alarm went off.

"What the frukx is going on now?" he mumbled under his breath. He punched in a sequence of keystrokes on the armrest of his seat, forcing the screen in front of him to bring up the video for the transport bay. More than likely, one of his specimens had gotten free of the tractor beam, not a huge worry with this latest batch. The planet Earth wasn't known for its deadly denizens. On the contrary, their creatures tended toward the docile side, especially the liquid-faring variety.

The bay, with its huge vats, appeared in his view screen, and he scanned the room, panning the camera in several directions. He didn't see anything, but then again, some of the critters he'd captured were quite small. Not like the knovakians with their forty astrometric-long tentacles. Those he'd had to sedate before capturing them for transport.

With a sigh of annoyance, he stood from his chair and stretched his bulky frame before stomping to the elevator that would take him to the lower level. He stopped just before entering and barked a command. "Proceed to the seventh planet in the quadrant and then drop into hyperspeed. Heading, the Jifnarian galaxy, third planet."

"Course locked." The smooth voice of his computer confirmed his orders. He grunted as he swung into the elevator and jabbed the button for the transport bay.

Going to wrestle a fish. The thought made him sigh. He'd come a long way from his career as a mercenary. His new life as a wrangler and transporter for rare species from undeveloped galaxies might bore the frukx out of him, but it sure beat getting his ass shot off every time he turned around. Of course, nothing could compare to the rush of a mission where he outsmarted security systems, pitted his skills against deadly guards, and came out ahead. But the life of a warrior for hire wasn't a long one, hence his career change.

However, no one had warned him that retirement would mean he'd end up bored out of his mind. He'd tried the life of leisure for a while, he'd certainly amassed enough credits to do so, but a male could only get drunk so many times and plow so many females before everything turned stagnant. So he bought a ship and started a new career—acquisitions specialist.

At least with his new business, he got to travel, fight the occasional reticent species, and kill off pirates. Those still stupid enough to engage him that was. His reputation preceded him, and now even the scum of the universe avoided him.

Time to change ships perhaps and fool them into thinking I'm new. He chuckled at the thought and made a mental note to have his business manager look into it. He could use the sport, and it always paid to keep one's skills sharp.

The door to the elevator slid open, disrupting his mental plan to fool pirates into playing, and he strode into the large transport bay.

"Lights," he barked.

The dim cavern immediately illuminated, and he strode through the tanks, heading toward the newest one to see what caused his alarm to still ring shrilly. He didn't bother masking the sound of his arrival, the heavy thump of his combat boots loud in the cargo bay. It wasn't like the specimens he'd caught could grow legs and run away. *What a shame.* He wouldn't have minded some form of entertainment.

Arriving at the recently filled vat, he peered around on the floor but found nothing around the base of the tank. He clambered up a ladder to reach the catwalks. He no sooner set foot on the metal grate than he saw a prone, wet lump.

"What the frukx is that?" It didn't look like the illustrations he'd seen of Earth's aquatic species. He wrinkled his nose at the stench, a briny, wet fish odor. Toeing the pale creature, he whipped his pistol out when it grunted.

What he'd mistaken for seaweed moved and then lifted until he found himself face to face with a face, a pale humanoid one. Big, brown eyes shot with red streaks blinked at him, and blue lips parted on a gasp.

"Holy shit. You're like Han Solo on crack," croaked the human. And with those strange words, the Earthling he'd accidentally abducted, slumped forward again. Its eyes rolled back in its head and its forehead smacked into the grated flooring.

"Ah, frukxn' crap." Tren braced his hands on his hips and grimaced down at the sodden mess. Kill the Earthling or keep it? He got the impression it was female, although given its contorted position and bedraggled state, it could have also been an effeminate male. Either way, he didn't want it. There wasn't a large market for Earthlings, not given their temperament. The females especially tended to cry all the time and descend into hysterics, especially when introduced to their new masters. Apparently, they took issue with the whole sold-as-a-sex-slave thing. It was why Tren stuck to creatures. They couldn't talk back.

I wonder if I can just drop her off somewhere on her planet. He discounted that idea almost immediately. One, he couldn't be bothered. And two, medical expeditions had learned their lesson after the Earthlings who came back after an abduction freaked, telling all who would listen about probes and needles. *Like we'd use such archaic forms of technology.* It made him sneer. Most of the civilized worlds considered Earth a barbarian planet, one bent on destroying its natural resources. It was why he'd made a trip to pick up specimens. At the rate they currently destroyed their oceans, he figured it wouldn't be long now before the whole planet expired, making what he'd grabbed a possible rarity.

Not that he cared about their fate. The galaxy had more than enough viable planets and sentient races. They wouldn't miss the loss of one backwards planet out in the far reaches.

But what to do about the Earthling? He raised his pistol to end the human's life, but hesitated. What had it meant when it called him Han Solo on crack? His translator didn't know what to make of it and, dammit, now he found himself curious.

I'll kill it after I find out. Decided, he holstered his gun and then crouched to grab the limp body. He rolled the human onto its back, and that's when he noticed the damage done to the female. And female she certainly was with her plentiful bosom spilling from the top of a soaking rag—only two breasts, though, instead of a lush four or five. He ignored her feminine attributes as he took in her twisted leg, broken in at least three places he'd wager.

I'm surprised she didn't scream her head off when she woke there for a moment. Probably shock kept her from noticing her injury. She'd certainly have plenty to say when she woke again—blubbering and gushing tears he couldn't abide. For a moment, he again debated just shooting her now before he had to put up with lunatic raving but stopped at the sight of her looking so utterly helpless. He cursed as he holstered his gun. He, the coldest killer in the known galaxies, couldn't kill her. *That's it. I need to go on a mission before I turn into a complete frukxning softy.* He'd let his contacts know he was back in business as soon as he got rid of his cargo, including one sure-to-be-annoying female.

He slid his hands under her plump frame and drew her toward him before standing with her cradled in his arms. With no effort on his part—he kept himself in impeccable shape—he carried her to the end of the walkway and the equipment lift. A short elevator ride later, he spilled onto an upper level where he kept his room and the medical chamber.

Curiosity made him peek at her while he carried her. Her skin appeared pale, extremely so, and beneath its surface he could see a fragile network of veins. He would have called her unblemished but noticed her skin appeared marred by a strange line of pale dots across the bridge of her nose. *That'll decrease her value*. She sported dark lashes and brows at odds with her pale-colored hair that streaked from a light gold to a dark brown. Her lips, an odd blue color, were full, and through their parted seam he could see white teeth, flat edged, making him wonder if perhaps her kind were herbivores. Her body filled his arms, opulent and soft, yet not obscenely so. The wet fabric she wore molded to the round fullness of her breasts and clung to her prominent nipples.

To his disbelief, his groin tightened at the sight. Apparently, he'd waited too long between brothel visits if this pale, sodden female could incite lust, especially considering she owned only two breasts—a common trait among her kind or a genetic abnormality?

Disgusted with himself and his interest in her as a copulating partner, he dumped her onto the diagnostic table in his medical room. The repair and diagnostic unit descended from the ceiling with a whir. Tren punched in a few commands on the device and then walked away, only to return a moment later when the machine beeped.

"Stupid machine. It can heal anything, but it can't stand wet clothes," he grumbled. He grasped the damp fabric adorning her frame and tore it in half before peeling it from her body. Womanly curves greeted him, and despite her dual mounds, he hungrily drank the sight of her in from the dark blush of her nipples to the brown thatch between her legs. His hand couldn't help but trace the round softness of her belly with its intriguing hole in the middle. He wondered what it was for and had to admit it made her body intriguing to behold, a fact his hardening cock agreed with.

With a curse at his lack of control, he whirled and stomped out of the chamber, letting the unit do its work. His clothes, damp and stinking of the Earth's ocean, required changing, and he proceeded to his chambers to do so. He dropped his soiled garments in the ship's cleansing unit before dressing in a clean and dry outfit. It was as he tucked his shirt into his pants that it occurred to him he'd have to clothe the female.

Or let her run around naked, his mind whispered with a dirty chuckle. His cock twitched at the thought. Tren tightened his lips into a thin line. *I am definitely visiting a brothel at my next stop.*

Not owning any feminine garments, he snagged a spare shirt and pants of his. He'd pick her up some clothes in one of his docking ports. Or he'd sell her naked, whichever he thought would fetch him a better price.

Knowing the medical unit would require a few more galactic units to complete its work, he went back to the command center, the spare clothes bundles under his arm. He wanted to do more research on Earthling females and discover ways of muzzling them because, with his luck, she'd probably end up the noisy, wailing type.

And all males know the only time a woman should speak is during sex when she screams our name.

Chapter Three

Megan regained consciousness slowly, a half smile curving her lips as her vivid dream of a space buccaneer kidnapping her for seduction slowly dissipated. *What an odd dream to have.* She opened her eyes and blinked as she stared up at some odd machine. Lights flashed, machinery whirred, and as she watched, a hole opened up and dropped a stream of goop on her.

"What the fuck?" She struggled to sit up but couldn't, which caused a mini panic attack. Hyperventilating, her head whipped from side to side, the only part of her she could move, looking for answers. No straps bound her arms, and when she lifted her head to peek, she saw nothing on her legs. Yet something, an invisible force, held her prone while the machine dropped icky stuff all over her body. Most disturbing of all, she wore not a stitch of clothing. *Who undressed me? And what did they do to my body?*

Memory of her abduction flooded her mind, and she closed her eyes with a groan. Apparently, the tall, dark pirate she vaguely remembered from her dream wasn't a figment of her imagination. He'd brought her aboard his ship and now prepared to… She cracked an eye open. Heal her? Probe her? Tenderize her body for eating? She hoped for the first option but wouldn't hold her breath.

Caught like a fly on sticky tape—until she could finagle her way out—she took stock of her situation. The burning pain in her leg and ribs seemed gone, numb with drugs? Or had the machine disabled her nerve endings? *Maybe to prevent me from screaming when they eat me alive?* She really shouldn't have watched that marathon of bad space movies with Cameron. Make that more like horror flicks about the different ways humans could die at alien hands.

Of her fatigue, not a trace remained, not even any soreness in her muscles from those hours of treading water. It made her wonder just how long she'd remained unconscious.

In order to keep herself from panicking as the machine marinated her skin in a variety of liquid slime, she turned her thoughts to her recollection of the alien, a twisted version of Han Solo. She wouldn't mind taking a peek at him again to see if he was as intriguing as she recalled. Delirious with pain, she'd gotten a brief impression of height, width, and piercing blue eyes. And surprise! He definitely hadn't expected to find her on his ship.

Heat suffused her, an unnatural warmth, and she craned her head as far as she could to see if the machine had set her body on fire. No flames licked at her skin, but the weird goop all over her body melted, and a moment later, the invisible force holding her let go.

Megan rolled off the table-like structure and peered around. As rooms went, this one sucked big time. Decorated in plain, off-white walls with no seams, or even a door, she found herself disappointed. So far, this space ship definitely wasn't living up to her expectations. Megan turned back to the table, the only object around, in time to see the machine that had gooped her recede into the ceiling.

Great. Now the room appeared even more barren. With nothing to intrigue her, and refusing to give in to panic—yet—she took a moment to take stock of herself, running her hands over her body, seeking any trace of soreness or abrasions. However, not only did she feel great, she also appeared better than new. Seriously. Whatever the machine had done, it not only healed her injuries but also took care of other imperfections, too. The scar from her emergency appendix surgery? Gone, along with the one on her knee from when she'd scraped it bad in her teens riding a bike and that spot on her shin she liked to nick when shaving. *Now if only it could have tightened my ass and tits up, too.* While she didn't mind their size, the jiggle when she ran was distracting.

Whole in body, unsure of her spirit, and with more questions than a cop, she prowled around the edges of the room, running her hands along the surface looking for a seam or something to press that would allow her to exit. She also really wished she could find something to wear. Somehow encountering alien life while in the buff didn't seem like it would put her at an advantage, so when she heard a whisper of sound behind her, she whirled while slapping one hand over her crotch and flinging the other across her boobs.

Given her generous size, that didn't accomplish much other than make her alien kidnapper open his eyes wide before laughing, an apparently universal sound.

"I fail to see the humor," she growled through gritted teeth. "Now, if you don't mind, I'd appreciate you turn around or, even better, run along to fetch me some clothes."

That shut him up even if he remained facing her. "Xfinew fika gdolpa?" He spoke to her in a guttural tongue that sent shivers dancing along her skin.

She ignored how his voice affected her and concentrated on the fact she didn't understand a damned thing he said. "I don't know what the hell you just said, so do you want to try again in English instead of whatever alien language you're using?" She tapped a bare foot as she glared at him imperiously. Naked or not, she refused to show fear, even if inside she quivered at the situation.

He snarled some foreign words before throwing a bundle at her and stalking out of the room. The package hit her as she watched in stunned amazement how the previously unseen door just slid across the opening, leaving the wall seamless again.

Unsure of when the annoyed alien freak would return, she perused the fabric package only to realize they were garments. She scrambled to get into the clothes, his, she surmised, judging by the size and style: a white tunic shirt that hung to her knees and pants that hugged her rounded ass but went well past her ankle. She sat down and rolled the bottoms until her feet peeked out. As attire went, she was well covered, if braless.

As she waited for the Martian to return, her mind took the time to dissect his appearance properly. First, immense didn't begin to describe him. The man had to tower over her by at least a foot or more, and at five foot eight, she wasn't some dainty little flower. And talk about wide. Holy freaking chest. She had only to look down at the shirt that draped her body to swallow in awe at the width of his torso. *Big from muscle or fat? Or does he have like alien parts hidden under there?*

She couldn't deny a curiosity to find out. Ignoring his body for a minute, she thought on his face and the color of his skin. *Purple, he's freaking purple.* Not a light pansy violet, but a deep rich mauve that made his almost opaque blue eyes pop. His dark hair, with its slight wave, hung almost to his shoulders, the color matching the neatly trimmed goatee on his square chin. He wore a silver ring in one nostril and another in his arched brow. His lips appeared black, but his teeth gleamed brightly—and pointed. *Definitely a carnivore with chompers like that.* And when he spoke in that strange gibberish, he rumbled low and sexy, a gruff voice to go with his tough-ass look. She vaguely recalled calling him Han Solo on crack, but she revised that to Johnny Depp in his pirate role commuted to space. Dark, dangerous, and wickedly hot looking. Given his alien characteristics, she had to wonder just what other surprises he hid other than his skin color and teeth, like maybe a forked dick or acidic jizz. She slapped a hand over her mouth before she could giggle aloud, not sure if he or some other E.T. watched her from some hidden camera.

Forget his good looks, she wasn't here on an intergalactic cruise to pick up sexy aliens—even if she couldn't deny curiosity. She'd narrowly escaped her last lover, and now that she had a second chance at life, she needed to swear off men—even hot space ones—for a while. A long while. *Hell, maybe I'll check out what it's like on the other side. Maybe I'd have better luck with another woman.* The idea didn't enthuse her.

With no warning, the wall slid open again, and her dark pirate stepped in, his clear eyes glittering. He tossed something small at her, and she lifted her hands to catch it—and missed. She'd never excelled at sports, outside the bedroom that was. Naked, she could keep up with any skinny bitch.

The little black object clattered to the floor, and she heard an exasperated sigh. "Well, excuse me for not being Miss Agile. You try getting almost drowned by your boyfriend, sucked into some spaceship by a tractor beam, and then having some weird machine experiment on you. I guarantee your reflexes would suck, too."

He didn't reply, just crossed his arms across his massive chest and inclined his head at the object on the floor. She stooped to pick it up and turned it in her hand, not recognizing the item at all. "What is it?"

Another sigh sounded, followed by movement. She flicked her gaze at him and sucked in a breath as she discovered him coming at her, almost seven feet of bristling, purple alien pirate. In a disgustingly girly reaction, she backed up. He growled, and in reflex, she growled back. Her response made his brows shoot up. She couldn't help the smirk that crossed her face as she threw him off balance.

In a lightning-quick move, his hand shot out toward her, and she squeaked before she dashed behind the table she'd woken up on.

"Don't come near me," she yelled. "You—you giant, purple weirdo."

"Kddwol sgewo." He spoke gibberish again and motioned her forward with his hand.

She snorted. Not likely. He snarled, baring his pointed teeth. With nothing to protect herself, she threw the black thing at him. He caught it with a blurring movement of his hand, and she gulped. He displayed remarkable reflexes. He moved around the table, and she shuffled her feet, keeping herself away.

It wasn't like her to act so cowardly, but truly, the guy—if an alien could be called a guy—was freaking huge, and he didn't look happy. She screamed when he leapt over the table and snagged an arm around her waist. She continued to shriek and thrash as he whirled her around. He yanked her back into his hard chest, his one arm an immovable anchor around her waist. His other hand fiddled at her ear, and she screamed. "Let go of me you freakish brute."

"Would you shut up, you annoying female, before I give into my first impulse to kill you."

As his words penetrated her panic, she stilled, her chest heaving. "I understood you," she whispered.

"Of course you did, silly human. If you hadn't panicked, like your kind are wont to do, I would have shown you how to insert the translator yourself."

"Well, how the hell was I supposed to know?" she snapped back. "It's not like I've ever met an alien before. In my world, we don't shove things in people's ears when we meet them for the first time."

"Yes, I am well aware of your planet's barbarian status," he retorted with a disgusted snort.

"What?" she sputtered. "Look who's calling the kettle black. I'd say you aren't that far from caveman status yourself."

"I knew I should have killed you," he grumbled from behind her.

It occurred to Megan that perhaps she should shut up for a moment before he acted on his words. The silence, though, made her aware of where she stood, more against whom. Pressed against her back, the alien heated her even through the fabric separating them. The palm pressed against her stomach branded her through the thin linen shirt and held her firmly against him. She wiggled in a sudden attempt to get away, but this served only to have him bring her closer, and her eyes widened as she felt something poking her in the back. *That better not be what I think it is.*

Instead of smartly shutting up, she took in a breath. "Oh, no fucking way. If you think I'm going to service you sexually, you are out of your mind. I don't bang guys I don't know, and that goes double for aliens. I don't care if you accidentally rescued me—"

He thrust her from him and snorted. "You think highly of yourself, female, if you think I would stoop to copulating with your pale form. Your mouth alone is enough to shrivel any man's cock."

Megan whirled and planted her hands on her hip. "Pale? I'm the one with some normal color here instead of freaking purple. And I'll have you know, my mouth has never received any complaints; on the contrary, my oral techniques are well known among my lovers." When his lips twitched into a partial grin, she grasped what she'd said and red heat rose up her neck to color her cheeks. However, she didn't cower or run. She stood straighter and faced him with a glare.

"Thank you for advising me of your aptitude. I shall be sure to add it to your list of skills when I auction you off at the first available port."

And with those words, he whirled on his heel and began walking away.

Auction? Oh, hell no. She steeled herself for battle and took off after him.

* * * *

Tren bristled with anger, not at the Earthling who'd amused him with her brave posturing and inane chattering, but at himself for his interest in finding out just how good her oral skills were. He had no interest in the barbarian creature, although, shoving his cock into her chatterbox would at least muffle the sound of her complaining for a while, something his turgid shaft urged him to try.

And there lay another issue—his attraction to her. It didn't help she'd gone from drowned, wretched-looking sea creature to feisty and surprisingly attractive female. Dry, her hair was streaked yellow and brown in a strangely attractive manner and curled slightly. Her backside, which he'd not noticed previously, was round and inviting. As for her two-breasted shape, he enjoyed the way her round breasts filled out the fabric of his shirt and how her nipples protruded through the fabric, begging for a mouth to suck them.

No. We do not play with the merchandise. Wait, that applied to virgin stock. From the way this one spoke, she was far from that state. *Although, she might end up as frozen food if she keeps haranguing me.* She followed close on his heels as he strode away in an attempt to escape her tirade.

"There will be no selling of me and my services," she screeched from behind him.

Tren ignored her and kept walking. What she wanted didn't even factor into his decisions.

"Ooh." Exasperation colored her exclamation, and a moment later, she attacked him, pummeling his back in a fury with her fists.

Seriously? He turned, and her blows rained on his rock-hard abdomen. He stared down at her while she vented her wrath, and only when she slowed did he drawl, "Done yet?"

She raised sparking brown eyes to his, and he couldn't help notice the pink flush on her cheeks. He found himself captivated by the redness of her lips, their natural color, he assumed, now that she'd warmed up. He missed seeing her knee, though, which connected with his cock with unerring accuracy.

"Now I am," she sassed, sounding all too pleased with herself.

Tren gritted his teeth through the burning pain, and before she could inflict more damage, he grabbed her and upended her over his shoulder.

"Put me down," she yelled, pounding his back with her fists.

"No."

"I will not let you rape me, you—you purple pirate!" she exclaimed.

"Like I said, I have no interest in your body. Not enough breasts for my liking. But lack of body parts or not, I'm going to sell you to the highest bidder." His words, delivered in a menacing tone, did nothing to halt her mouth.

"You can't do this to me. I demand you bring me back to my planet. I will not be sold like-like an object."

"Silence," he roared, smacking her bottom with the flat of his hand to grab her attention. When she screeched in rage, he smacked her again and again until she quieted. A shame because he would have enjoyed slapping it some more, perhaps naked. She did have the most delectable bottom. "Finally, some quiet. Now listen up, Earthling. Firstly, we're not even in your star system any longer, so returning you to your home world is not an option, which, believe me, I am already regretting. Secondly, I'm beginning to think, unless I muzzle you or remove your tongue, I'll never have any luck selling you. Men like their females docile and biddable. And quiet, very, very quiet. A lesson you might wish to learn. And three, my ship, my rules."

"Your rules suck."

Tren's jaw dropped in surprise at her reply. Did this female not own common sense? Only idiots antagonized him—and never more than once. He made sure of that. "Anyone ever tell you that you don't know when to shut up?"

"All the time, but let me ask you, how would you feel if your boyfriend tried to kill you and then you got kidnapped by an alien who wants to sell you? Would you just give up?"

Then, to his horror, she burst into tears.

"Oh, no. No tears. I won't tolerate that. You stop crying this instant," he ordered.

She just sobbed louder.

At a loss, Tren, who'd reached the command center at last, dropped her into his chair and stood back to survey her. His captive smirked at him, not a trace of tears to be seen on her face. She'd faked it.

A grudging admiration at her spirit tugged him, but annoyance at her drama tempered it. "I see even Earthling females are prone to the same dramas as all females the universe over." Her reply to his disgruntled observation? She blew him a noisy kiss and flashed her middle finger at him, which probably meant something back on her planet but just gave him an urge to bite her digit—then suck it.

Pushing aside thoughts of places he'd like to nibble on her frame, he discovered a curiosity about some of her earlier words. "Why did your male companion choose to kill you? Was it because you wouldn't shut up?"

"No," she replied, her spine straightening as he intentionally goaded her. "He wanted my money. Stupid me, I didn't know he was a con man until he decided he no longer needed me. He pushed me off a boat and left me to drown."

Strangely, the actions of her male partner angered him. Not that he let it show. "Lucky me, I now get his botched remains. I warn you right now you'd better start behaving because, if I decide to kill you, I will succeed." He gave her his most dangerous look and waited to see the fearful respect he'd grown accustomed to.

She stuck her tongue out at him, and Tren almost went crossed eyed at her temerity. "Go ahead," she taunted.

"Are you insane, female?" he roared. "I told you to behave or else."

"Why bother? You already said you intend to sell me," she accused. "That's not very nice, you know."

Tren shrugged. "Niceness doesn't enter into it at all. It's just business. You were a part of my catch, and I can't just release you; it wouldn't make financial sense when I can fetch a small price for the trouble you're going to incur."

"What trouble? Are the space police going to come after you for abducting me?" Her tone and eyes brightened at the prospect, and Tren almost laughed.

He controlled himself, keeping a serious mien plastered to his visage. He did, however, snort before replying. "Policing is for those that are a part of the universal coalition. Your backward planet doesn't count, and everything on it, including its people, are fair game. Most slavers just can't be bothered with your kind because of your mental instability."

"Our what?" she sputtered.

"Screaming hysterics and lack of basic understanding of how the universe works." He shrugged. "Actually, kind of like the behavior you're currently exhibiting." He moved sideways and avoided the foot she swung his way.

"Well, at least we're not rude, overbearing jerks," she retorted.

Tren growled at her and bared his teeth. To his annoyance, she didn't even flinch. "Do you know how easily I could kill you?"

She rolled her eyes. "Oh, please. Save the big, bad routine for someone more gullible. If you didn't murder me after I kicked you in the balls, then you're not going to for just talking."

A scowl crossed his face at her reasoning, and to his amazement, she laughed, a rich throaty sound that made her lips curve enticingly and her eyes dance. It also made his cock swell with interest. He didn't like it one bit. *How am I supposed to make her respect me if she finds my threats amusing?* He'd never run into that issue before. Most beings cowered, fainted, or wet themselves when he turned his displeasure their way.

He needed some space from her and the contrary emotions she evoked. "I've got work to do. Don't touch anything." He barked the command at her, but she just continued to grin in a way he found disturbing. To ensure she didn't attempt to drive them into the nearest star, he tapped a panel on the wall by the elevator and locked the console to voice command only—his voice—then left. To his surprise—and odd disappointment—she didn't say a thing to stop him.

Good. It's about time she gave that tongue of hers a rest. Although he could think of other ways she could exercise it. Ways that made his cock strain the crotch of his pants.

Chapter Four

Alone, Megan drummed her fingers on the armrest of the chair and looked around with interest. For some reason, she'd expected a bigger command center for the ship. However, the actual space rivaled that of her spare bedroom with less furniture. She knew the ship was immense from her glimpse of the cargo bay and how much floor they'd traversed when he'd carried her upside down—those long legs of his had an immense stride—the impression compounded as they got on an elevator to change floors for God's sake.

However, sizable as it all seemed, the one thing his ship seemed to lack was other people, beings, aliens, whatever she wanted to call them. Despite his purple color, she found herself hard-pressed to think of him as an extraterrestrial. He oozed too much testosterone and chauvinism for that. *Just like a man back home.*

It occurred to her she should probably be more upset about her current situation—hysterical screaming and hyperventilating came to mind—but honestly, after the shock of her attempted murder, this space adventure she found herself on came as kind of a relief. And it wasn't as if anyone would miss her; she had no family left to care about her, part of the reason she was such an easy mark for preying men. She worked from home as a web programmer and analyst, so no coworkers existed to wonder where she'd gotten to. As for friends, Cameron made sure to estrange her from them. *Grooming me for my eventual midnight swim, the jerk.*

What truly pissed her off wasn't her currently odd situation but the fact that Cameron had probably made it back to dock by now and probably celebrated her demise at his hands. *Spending my money, the asshole.* She wanted to go back just so she could kill him herself.

While thoughts of revenge and annoyance at Cameron sustained her, the more immediate concern was her eventual fate. Despite her captor's threats, she didn't get the impression he'd actually abuse her, even if he kept threatening to kill or sell her. His smacks on her ass had stung, but given his size and evident strength, he'd obviously held back. Not like some of her previous boyfriends who'd turned violent for less provocation. *I honestly don't think the purple pirate will hurt me.* A possibly dumb intuition based on nothing more than gut instinct, which in her case had shown itself as rather unreliable in the past.

I have such a great track record with men. If they're not out to screw me, they're fucking around on me, trying to beat me, or, in my newest scenario, murdering me. She never put up with any of their shit, of course, but the pain of their betrayals still hurt. *Is it so much to ask for a guy who'll like me for who I am, outspoken, curvy, and all?*

Maybe she should consider allowing her captor to sell her as a sex slave, an object of value to someone, even if alien. Allow herself to become someone who gave and received sexual pleasure. *I'm good at that. I could become a first-class courtesan and have my owner shower me with presents,* an interesting fantasy for someone else. However, knowing her penchant for giving orders and stating her mind, it seemed an unlikely scenario in her case.

Alone and in need of something to occupy herself, she hopped up from the chair and prowled the control center, or so she assumed even given the sparse decor. Unlike the *Star Trek* films and shows she'd watched, there existed a definite lack of cool flashing lights, buttons, and levers. Just a lot of blank wall space with faint scribbles, a chair, and a big window-like screen that showed nothing, not even her reflection.

Boring.

She leaned against the screen and tried to peer through it, wondering if perhaps it acted as a two-way glass.

"Command console locked. Please speak to confirm identity."

Megan reeled back at the feminine voice that spoke from thin air. When nothing happened and no one appeared, she lightly touched the screen with a finger.

"Command console locked. Please speak to confirm identity."

This was more like it. A voice activated computer. Cool. "Um, hi, I'm Megan."

"Invalid voice entry."

"So whose voice will work?" Megan spoke aloud, but the computer didn't reply. Her abductor probably had it keyed for only him.

Foiled in that area, she wandered around touching various panels where she found symbols, some of which caused the computer to relay the same command, some of which did nothing. She also tried to figure out how to open the door to the elevator thing but ended up kicking the wall in aggravation and stubbing her toes.

Annoyed, she threw herself at the wall with a frustrated yell, pummeling it with her fists. When it suddenly slid open, she stumbled forward into a brick wall with steadying hands.

"Are you done abusing my vessel?" said her purple captor in his low, sexy voice.

A shiver skated down her spine, and it had nothing to do with fear. Her hands, sprawled across his chest, registered a steady thump, like a heartbeat; of course, it was on the wrong side of his torso and lower, but it still made him seem more human. Awareness of his body and an answering call in her lower tummy stunned her more, though. *Attracted to a purple slave trader with pointed teeth? Am I completely insane?*

Realizing he waited for her to speak, she sprang on the first thought that came to mind, other than asking him to remove his shirt so she could inspect him. "I'm bored and hungry," she complained, pushing back from him. She shot him a mutinous look as she crossed her arms over her chest, mostly to hide her erect nipples that seemed determined to catch his attention.

"I didn't realize it was your people's custom to throw a tantrum like a young'un."

Her chin tilted stubbornly at his rebuke. "Maybe if you hadn't locked me up with nothing to do I wouldn't have to resort to childish tactics to get some attention."

She could have sworn she saw a glint of humor momentarily light his eyes. "Oh, you have my attention. Don't blame me, though, if you don't like it." He bared his teeth at her, and she rolled her eyes.

"Enough with the trying to intimidate me. I'm no use to you dead, so unless you're planning on starving me as some sort of punishment, I need food."

"I have better ways of chastising you." His eyes roved her body sensually. Megan couldn't help the bolt of heat that speared her cleft.

She pretended to not understand his sexual innuendo. "Could you beat me after you feed me?"

"Follow me and I shall provide sustenance. Perhaps it will improve your ill disposition." He smirked as he stepped back into the elevator, and as she entered the tight space facing him, she threw a dirty look at him for his remark. He leaned around her, and she sucked in a breath, expecting retaliation, only to release it when she realized he simply wanted to push a button.

It occurred to her as the door slid shut behind her she didn't know if her space pirate had a name. Somehow purple people eater didn't seem apt. "My name is Megan, by the way, or do you not name the merchandise you're going to sell?"

She could have sworn his lips twitched before his grim façade took over again. "I'm Tren, and I name all the things I sell. New hover car. Relaxing retreat. Night at the Red Vulva. You know, that type of thing."

It was her turn for her lips to quirk. "Touché. So, I have to ask, if my people are such barbarians, how is it you know our language?"

"I don't, the translator does. It is standard protocol for the devices to be programmed with all known languages, defunct or not. Although I believe the version for your planet might be somewhat out of date given some of your expressions aren't translating."

Megan inclined her head in understanding. "Pop culture references I'll bet."

"And this Han Solo I heard you mention before, he is a pop culture?" His clear blue eyes bored into hers as the elevator stopped, and she almost fidgeted at his intense look.

"He's a movie character. From *Star Wars*." At his blank look, she laughed. "I don't think I can explain this without you seeing the actual movie. But, basically, your whole bad-ass buccaneer look was first done by Harrison Ford who played Han Solo in the *Star Wars* trilogy."

The brows of her captor drew together. "I am not an actor."

She rolled her eyes. "Well, duh. I'm just saying, at first glimpse, you reminded me of him in that role. But don't worry. Now that I've really gotten to look at you without the whole pain and exhaustion thing messing me up, I've changed that comparison to Johnny Depp in *Pirates of the Caribbean*. Except you have whiter teeth, pointier, too."

His lips tightened at her words. "Nothing you've just said makes much sense. I am myself, and while there are those who would try to copy me, I am unique." He stepped from the elevator into a long hall, his back stiff.

Megan laughed. It appeared as if Tren, her purple pirate, was offended. "I never said you weren't unique." He swiveled to peer back at her and shot her a dark glare. She smirked, and with a shake of his head, he turned back again. "Just forget it. So where are we going?"

"My quarters."

Megan stopped walking. "Excuse me. When I said I was hungry, I meant for food, not sex."

He craned to look at her over his shoulder, and she definitely couldn't mistake his slow grin this time. It transformed his face and made her heart stutter. "Who said anything about sex? It's where the food replicator is located. Although, since you keep offering, I am not averse to testing the merchandise after our meal."

Megan's mouth rounded into an O of surprise. "Like hell."

"I would assume you mean no. But do not blame me for offering. You are the one who keeps referring to intercourse. I was just trying to meet your obviously insatiable needs." He eyed her frame up and down in a slow perusal that ignited a slow burn between her legs.

She pressed her thighs tight together. "I need another lover like I need a hole in my head. No thank you. And I am not some kind of nymphomaniac." Even if the current conversation was making her hot.

"If you say so," he drawled as he led the way into a large suite, which, of course, held a massive round bed.

Megan ignored it, afraid any comment would lead him to believe she wanted to test its springs—which her pussy certainly did—but went against the grain. While she enjoyed a healthy sexual appetite, she had one teensy tiny requirement in her partners. She had to at least like them.

She wandered around the space, noting the table bordered by chairs that appeared made of rubber. A shelving unit built into the wall held strange objects, figurines of creatures but unlike any she'd imagined. One appeared a mix of fairy and a dragon in a rainbow of colors. Another, a voluptuous woman with five boobs, waved four arms.

"Are these real creatures?" she asked, running her finger across their varied surfaces.

"Keepsakes from some of my more notable conquests," he boasted.

She snatched her hand back and whirled with wide eyes. "You fucked all of them?"

He frowned at her. "If you mean had sex, then yes. But that's only a fraction of the females I've been with and, like I said, the most memorable."

"Great, I'm stuck on a ship with man whore," she snorted with disgust, although she couldn't deny a certain curiosity. *Exactly how knowledgeable is he about the female form?*

"I am not paid to pleasure my partners. However, if the need is great and I am not in the mood to woo, then I will recompense a female for her time."

"Great. I made it to space and met my first alien, only to discover men all over the universe are pigs."

Tren's brow knitted into a frown. "I do not like your tone or implication. My method is the one most widely followed through the known universe. How do your people handle their sexual needs?"

"We date. You know, go out to dinner, maybe see a movie. Then, if we like each other, we go to bed."

Tren laughed, a short barking sound. "So instead of exchanging credits, you are purchased for a meal or an evening of entertainment. I see no difference other than your females can be cheaply bought. And at least my conquests don't try to kill me after we're done."

His reference to her boyfriend's attempted murder rankled, and Megan glared at him. "I'm really starting to dislike you."

"Good. I hate clingy females."

With that rejoinder, he turned his back on her and fiddled with something on the wall above the table. A moment later, an odd aroma tickled her nose.

Curious, she stepped forward and saw two plates, the steam still rising, resting on the table. "What is that?"

"Food."

She slid into the rubber chair, which molded to fit her bottom and almost caused her to scream. When she realized her seat wasn't about to swallow her, she relaxed enough to poke at the purple and green stuff on her plate, interspersed with white marble things. "What kind of food?"

"The kind that won't kill you, so eat."

Using a pair of silver rods, much like chopsticks, he dug into his meal. With trepidation, and, yes, a fear of food poisoning, she followed suit. To her surprise, she didn't immediately spit it back out. Whatever the goop on her plate was, it tasted pretty good. She ate with relish, the only dinner sounds consisting of them chewing and swallowing.

As her hunger eased, curiosity prompted her to question him. "So, you're obviously not human. What exactly are you?"

He swallowed before answering. "I am Kulin, a mighty warrior race superior to your own."

"Well, you're definitely more conceited, I'll give you that. As for superior, I'd say the jury is out on that one." She ignored the dirty look he shot her way and continued on her quest for answers. "So are there like a lot of other alien-type dudes out in the galaxy? I mean, other than your skin color and teeth, you look kind of human, so is that the norm?"

"The universe contains many varied life forms. While bipeds are the most common, it would be ignorant to assume that most creatures are like yourself. Especially given your lower status on the evolutionary scale compared to the more advanced and genetically enhanced civilizations."

"Wow, you really are a jerk. Apparently, when it comes to manners, you're not so advanced, Mr. My-shit-smells-better-than-yours." His furrowed brow at her insult was his reply. A portion of his statement caught her attention, though. "Wait a second? Did you say genetically enhanced? What's that mean?"

"Some of us choose to expand upon the abilities we are born with. It's almost a standard procedure along with embryo manipulation to ensure not only physical perfection, but mental astuteness as well."

"Great, you're not only a purple freaking space pirate, but a *Mutant X* one on top of it." Once again, she pretended not to see his annoyed expression. She actually wanted to ask him a whole bunch of other questions, such as whether he had any super powers, but she wasn't sure how far his patience would stretch before he shut her down. Prudence dictated that she leave the subject of his genetic aberrations for later to hit the most important query first. "So where exactly are we going?"

"Somewhere I can auction you off."

She frowned at him. "And where would that be?"

"The first planet we come across that offers that service."

Irritation at him and his plan in general made her flick—accidentally of course—a piece of food in his direction. The jerk opened his mouth and caught it. Intrigued, she flung another piece. Arching a brow at her, he caught it again with a snapping jaw. Megan didn't, however, manage the same with the chunk he tossed at her.

She wiped it off her cheek, all the while glaring at him. He just grinned back and continued to eat.

No longer hungry—and petulant he'd beaten her at her own game—she pushed the plate away and looked around but didn't spot what she wanted. "You got anything to drink?"

Without pausing in his meal, he slapped his hand sideways and pressed the wall a few times, causing a faint glow to appear each time. A moment later, a compartment slid open and out slid two glasses, more like pitchers considering their size.

She dragged one toward her and peered into its ruby-colored depths. "Please tell me this is wine."

"If you mean an alcoholic beverage, then yes."

Just what she needed. Megan took a sip and wondered at his idea of alcohol, given how smoothly the stuff slid down her throat. Thirsty, she took several swallows before she noticed him watching her.

"You may want to imbibe more slowly. The Kijar you drink can prove quite potent for the uninitiated."

She blew him a raspberry. "Bah. I can drink like a fish." Her boast came out slightly slurred, and she giggled. "Fish. I guess since you caught me in your space net, I'm like some kind of m-mermaid." She howled at her own joke. She glanced over at him and saw his puzzled look. It set her off again, and she fell off the chair laughing. She scrambled to her feet, swayed, and took another swig of the yummy wine.

"I think you've had enough."

She slapped the mug back down. "Did not." She shook her finger at him. "You're just a sp-spoilsport." She giggled at his stern look. She went to grab the wine, but he slid the mug out of her reach. She lunged at it but ended up missing it and losing her balance. Not a big deal since she landed on his lap.

His arms steadied her, and she thought she heard him sigh. She twined her arms around his neck. "You smell good," she announced, sniffing his neck.

"You're drunk."

"Am not," she announced. She squirmed in his lap, and he groaned. Sensing his distraction, Megan snatched her mug and drained the contents. Her whole body glowed with warmth, and she twisted back to smile at him.

"You're not bad looking for a purple dude." She twined a finger in some of his hair, surprised at its softness.

He tilted his head away, freeing his lock of hair. "I believe you should rest to sleep off the effects of the drink."

"Ooh, time for bed." She hopped off his lap, staggered, and caught her balance. She veered toward the bed and collapsed on it, giggling. She rolled onto her back and peered over at him. "Aren't you coming?"

* * * *

Tren didn't know if he should throttle the Earthling or join her in the bed. Aggravating, mouthy, outspoken, stupidly brave and fascinating. He'd never met a female like her, and he'd yet to decide if he liked her or wanted to kill her. Right now, his body knew what it wanted—her naked with her thighs spread wide so he could plow her. He'd done enough research to know their sexual organs were compatible, and he was tempted to see just how far that compatibility went—and how good her vaunted oral skills were.

She sprawled, with a grin, on his bed and beckoned him with a crooked finger. While he recognized her brazenness resulted from overindulgence, he couldn't deny her allure.

"You're drunk," he stated flatly, but his claim did nothing to stop his cock from swelling.

"And horny." She enhanced her statement with a grope of her breasts, squeezing their plump shape.

A part of him urged him to show some control and turn away from her display. But quite honestly, he was enjoying it too much. He did try to caution her again, though. "You will yell at me when you come to your senses."

"I'll yell more if you don't get over here." She patted the bed beside her.

A male had only so much endurance. Tren shrugged and stood from the table to approach the bed. He loomed over her, and she licked her lips as she stared up at him with heavily lidded eyes.

"Take off your shirt," she ordered. "I've been dying to see what you're hiding under there."

Tren stripped the white linen off and almost took his pants off, too, at the appreciation in her gaze.

"Good grief," she whispered. "Even your abs have abs."

His chest swelled at the awe in her tone. "I take it you are pleased?"

She struggled to her knees and ran her hand across his chest, her soft skin leaving pleasant tingles where it touched. Tren sucked in a breath when she placed both palms against him. She leaned forward and brushed her lips on his skin, a scalding mark that shot straight to his groin. Unlike the males of her kind, he did not possess nipples—a wasted characteristic on a male in his opinion. But his chest wasn't without adornment.

She found his silver ringed piercings, a pair on each side, penetrating his upper pectorals. She tugged them and grinned. "These are hot." She leaned forward and ran her tongue around the metal, and Tren closed his eyes at the intense sensation.

Warming and wetting them, she toyed with the rings, and Tren wondered if she knew how sensitive they were to any type of touch. Whether she did or not, she played them with expertise. She alternated between pulling and licking his erogenous zone.

Arousal raged through his body, rendering him impatient, a distinctly new sensation for him. He placed his hands around her waist and lifted her until they were eye level, hers glazed with a burgeoning passion. She parted her lips, and he expected her to speak—it seemed her habit to forever chatter—but she finally put her lips to better use, pressing them against his with a soft sigh. The sensation proved electric.

Tren folded her tight to him, his mouth plundering hers in a sensual kiss that rendered his breath ragged. Her hands crept up to slide through his hair, dragging his face closer. The feel of her tongue slipping between his lips made him groan as he met it, thrust for thrust. He grazed his pointed teeth along its length, and she mewled into his mouth.

Her lower body pressed against him, and he dropped one hand to grab her thigh and wrap it around his waist. Quickly understanding, she twined her other leg around him as well, bringing her covered sex up against his throbbing cock.

She keened, the sound vibrating against his lips as she gyrated her hips against his hard appendage. He slid his hands lower to cup her buttocks, aiding her in grinding against him as their mouths continued to mesh wetly. The taste of her drove him wild, and her passionate response almost disintegrated his control. When she sucked his tongue into her mouth, grazing her own flat-edged teeth along it before biting it, he almost threw her down to have his way with her.

I am a warrior. I have more control than an animal. Barely, he had to grudgingly amend.

In order to regain some of his senses, he tore his mouth from hers, but the vixen tortured him further when she bent her head back, exposing her throat, a true act of trust and eroticism among his kind. Unable to resist, he latched onto her tender skin with his lips whilst nipping her lightly with his sharp teeth. He fought against an urge to bite harder, to mark her with his distinctive dentition.

Among his people, in times past, such an act would act as a permanent claim, declaring to all she belonged to him. He growled at the primitive impulse, unsure of why it even crossed his mind but determined not to give in. He moved his teeth away from the temptation she so unwittingly offered and sealed his lips back to her eager mouth.

She clawed at his shoulders, her motions against him frantic and driving him wild with arousal. He thrust his hips toward her, the molten heat of her core affecting him even through their layers of clothing. Her gasping cries came faster and faster, their lower body friction reaching a fever pitch.

With a final short scream, her body went tense against his, and his sensitive cock felt the quivering of her cleft muscles. She'd found her first pleasure, and Tren's chest swelled in pride. *I made her climax and without even taking her clothes off.* Her erotic and responsive nature made him eager to ready her for the next orgasm.

"That freakin' rocked," she whispered as she laid her head on his shoulder. He would have responded, but the sound of her soft snore made his jaw drop in incredulity.

She fell asleep?

Not believing it, he pried her from his body and placed her on the bed. She squirmed for a second on the covers, tucking her knees up slightly, but her eyes remained closed, and Tren ran a hand through his hair in disbelief.

Now what am I supposed to do with this? He peered down at his swollen cock ruefully. Even he wouldn't stoop to taking a woman while she slept, obviously passed out from not just orgasm but overindulgence as well.

However, while his morals dictated he only plow conscious females, it didn't say anything about masturbating beside them. He kicked off his boots and stripped off his pants, his swollen prick springing forth. He debated lying beside her or even going into the ablutions chamber to take care of his need, but for some reason he wouldn't examine, he wanted to look upon her as he stroked himself.

Holding out his palm, he spit on it before he gripped his shaft. The liquid provided a natural lubricant for his self-caress. Sliding his hand back and forth along his swollen length, he watched her, her red lips pouting as she slept, her cheeks still flushed from passion. He groaned at the way her breasts strained against the fabric of his shirt, and, most enticing of all, the lingering scent of her arousal.

He fisted his cock, squeezing his hard length while imagining the pale human on her knees, her breasts offered up as a bed for his seed. Perhaps she would flick out her tongue to lap at the head of his prick. The tantalizing visual image drove him over the edge. With a grunt, he shot his creamy load onto her shirt.

Sated, if not completely satisfied, he then debated what to do. He wasn't in the habit of spending his sleeping time with females. He preferred to slumber alone. However, his vessel wasn't exactly equipped for guests, and given her propensity for trouble, he didn't want to leave her alone. Plausible excuses, even if a part of him knew better. He wanted to remain with her, and he didn't understand the reason why.

I guess she stays in my bed for now. But what had to leave was the soiled shirt she now wore. He maneuvered her limp body until he'd tugged the fabric off. She never woke, and he paused to enjoy for a moment the view of her breasts, her pink nipples puckering in the air. *Perhaps the next time she over imbibes, I'll start with those first.* He didn't question the natural ease with which he assumed a second encounter.

About to crawl into bed, he stopped. She looked odd wearing just his pants, and besides, they were damp with the lingering traces of her climax. He tugged those off her as well, grinning as he imagined her reaction when she woke. *If I'm lucky, she'll jump up to harangue me and treat me to a show of her breasts jiggling.* A chuckle on his lips, he clambered into the bed beside her, nude as well, and tugged the covers up over both their forms.

"Lights off." The room darkened, and he lay on his back, much too aware of her lying beside him. He tossed one way then tossed the other. He rolled onto his back and sighed. Sleep eluded him, and he didn't need to look too far to find the cause.

What was it about this barbarian female that drew him? Allowed her to get away with audacities that he'd killed others over in the past? He could name so many things about her he disliked, and yet, he couldn't kill her. Frukx, he couldn't even toss her out of his bed. Did she exude some kind of alien hormone that made him grudgingly spare her? Impossible, given how thoroughly his medical unit had examined her. And yet, here she lay, quiet for the moment, but that would surely only last until the sleeping period ended. And he could just imagine the rant she'd subject him to. A grin spread over his face as he looked forward to sparring with her.

A rustle of fabric gave him only a moment's warning before a lush, naked body rolled onto his. He held his breath as she snuggled into his side, her arm draping over his chest while her thigh flung over his. Her warm breath tickled the skin of his torso, and for a moment, he thought of shoving her away. He'd dumped more than one female out of bed when she'd attempted to cuddle. Yet, still in the grips of some strange mood, he instead wrapped his arms around her to tuck her in closer, and before he knew it, he slept as well.

Chapter Five

Megan woke with a pounding head and a thick tongue.

What happened? Well, other than almost dying and getting kidnapped by a hunky alien pirate. Those parts she remembered in glaring detail.

The last thing she recalled involved dinner and that yummy tasting wine. Then…

Oh, god. She groaned aloud and something shifted under her cheek, something solid and skin covered. Her eyes popped open, and she stifled a second groan as she discovered herself plastered to one very large, purple body. Although mortified, she couldn't help noticing how deliciously solid he felt. Flashes of the previous evening careened through her mind—mainly her riding him like an overdressed cowgirl and getting off. Her cheeks heated with embarrassment, and her cleft moistened in interest. *Oh, shit. I threw myself at him like some slut.* And loved it. Even now she could remember the heated passion, the powerful feel of him, then nothing after her climax achieved from just rubbing against him. She squirmed, and another fact became glaringly evident.

I'm naked, and yet I don't recall stripping.

The only conclusion to draw from her undressed status was they'd done it and she didn't remember a thing. She didn't know which bummed her more: her appalling actions while drunk or the fact that she couldn't conjure up a single recollection from her first—and only, dammit—bout of alien probing. Her snide mind—and wakening libido—wondered if she could ask for a repeat. *No!* That was crazy thinking. There would be no second round. The pirate did plan to sell her, after all, and she did have some self-respect, now that she was sober anyway.

The chest under her cheek shifted, and she ended up rolled onto her back with a very happy-to-see-her alien poking at the juncture of her thighs. His powerfully built arms held him up at an angle that kept his chest off hers, but his groin lay snug up against the apex of her thighs. Hot tingles at his proximity made her body thrum with wakening desire, and she almost let her legs part to see his version of a good morning. However, a lack of coffee and pigheadedness made her clamp them shut tighter instead. During her inner battle with her libido, he peered down at her, his face wearing a serious mien at odds with his tousled hair.

"You are awake." He stated the obvious.

"No kidding." She didn't move for fear of inadvertently titillating him and giving her body more ideas than it needed. Already, the heat radiating from his body, suspended over hers, made her nipples pebble and her cleft moisten further.

"You appear displeased." He didn't seem surprised.

"You took advantage of me," she accused.

His dark brows shot up, and his lip curled into a sneer. "In your dreams, Earthling. You mauled me. I simply took what you offered, make that almost begged me to take."

The jerk would point out that fact. "I was drunk, and you took advantage to fuck me."

He snorted as he rolled off her, and her body immediately mourned the loss of his warmth. "If you are implying I plowed your sex, then you're mistaken. I'm not into unconscious females."

"Then how do you explain my nakedness? While I remember kissing you, as I recall, I wore clothes at the time."

"I stripped you for your comfort. Next time I'll just dump your drunken carcass onto the floor and keep the bed to myself."

She didn't like the callous way he acted and refused to admit she might have brought it on herself with her accusations. "You're a jerk." *Who obviously didn't like what he saw enough to take advantage.* She didn't understand why that bothered her. She should have celebrated the fact she remained relatively untouched.

"Shrew."

They glared at each other over the expanse of the bed, and that's when her eyes strayed, catching on to the fact that she currently had one very big, naked alien to peruse, and—*oh my freaking god*—he appeared hotter than she fuzzily recalled.

Muscles delineated his upper body, and she sucked in a breath at the sight of the rings piercing his skin where she noticed a lack of nipples. He'd quite enjoyed the way she'd tugged and sucked on his pectoral ornaments, and her pussy moistened further in remembrance. She couldn't help her eyes from straying down his rock-hard abs—that owned their own little abs—down to the vee of his hips. Apparently he lacked modesty since he stood proudly with no attempt at covering himself. She let her gaze wander even lower to his hairless groin. From between his heavily muscled thighs, his massive cock jutted, stained a dark mauve color while its thick head blushed pink. And that's when she noticed the freakiest thing.

"Oh, my fucking god, you've been neutered!"

"What?" he barked, planting his hands on his hips, which drew even more attention to his crotch area—his ball-less crotch area.

"Neutered, spayed, or whatever the hell you call it when you've had your balls chopped off. Dear god, don't tell me that's how you aliens practice birth control?" Megan couldn't help the horror that seeped into her voice. *And he called humans barbaric.*

Wider and wider his eyes grew, his throat working soundlessly. When he finally managed to utter something, it emerged a cross between a snort and laughter. "You are absolutely insane. What are you talking about?"

"Your balls. You know, the two round things that hang under your dick. What happened to them? Did they take them from you when they sliced off your nipples?"

A pair of purple hands came up to cover his face, and his shoulders shook as he mumbled under his breath.

Megan leaned forward, ignoring her own nudity as she got closer in case he needed a shoulder to cry on. Her observation might have lacked diplomacy, but she could at least be kind about the fact he found himself maimed.

"There, there. Don't cry. I'm sorry. It's just, how awful for you that you've been mutilated. Did it hurt? Can you still function, like, you know, a man down there?" Judging by his rapidly dwindling cock, she had to wonder at his ability to come. Perhaps an inability to ejaculate was why he'd not molested her when he had the perfect chance.

Noise came from behind his hands, and it sounded suspiciously like laughter. She frowned at him.

"Earthling," he managed to sputter in a choked voice. "You should have chosen a career in the comedic arts." He peeled his hands away, and she saw his face twisted in a rictus of mirth. "Those balls, as you call them, are tucked into my body, as is the case with all of my kind. Only a less evolutionized race would keep their seed sacs out in the open where they are vulnerable to damage. As for nipples, females have nipples, not males. Why would we? We are not the ones who feed the young. There is nothing wrong with me. You, however, you're one to talk about deformity with your two breasts and that hole in your stomach."

Megan gaped at him. "Deformity?" She grabbed her heavy breasts and held them up. "Do these look deformed to you? I think my tits are perfectly beautiful, thank you. And as for my belly button, all humans have one. It's because we're normal."

"Says you," he retorted. Despite his assertion she was far from perfect, he couldn't hide the fact his cock rapidly re-inflated at her self-grope.

A glaring match ensued as they tried to stare each other down—his prick straining and her pussy soaking—and they might have remained at an impasse for a while had the ship's computer not interrupted.

"Approaching way station, Lokihaj. Recommend docking for refueling and repair of malfunctioning thruster."

Tren growled as he turned to stalk away, and Megan sucked in a breath at the view of his toned back and ass, purple perfection that made her hands itch to stroke and pinch. *Maybe I should have handled this morning differently?* In other words, held her tongue, let him probe her with that purple dick of his, and then drawn a silent conclusion on his prowess, balls or not.

Pride wouldn't let her call him back to apologize, and he seemed hell bent on ignoring her, which kind of miffed her. *I mean, if he really liked what happened last night and what he saw, shouldn't he be trying harder to get another piece?* His cock sure seemed willing to give it a go. Instead, the pirate slapped his hand on the wall, and a compartment opened from which he pulled clean shirts and pants, a set of which he flung at her without looking. Another slap and a new door opened, and he walked out of the room.

Megan tugged on the garments as she wished fervently for a toilet, followed by a shower and a comb to freshen herself. She'd understood enough of the computer's message to understand they'd reached some kind of civilization. Not sure how this helped her, but determined to have a say in her fate, she strode into the adjoining room after Tren.

She found herself in a white haven she guessed passed as a bathroom, given it had some kind of shower enclosure and a long counter with a pile of his clothes. What she really wanted to know, as did her bladder, was where the toilet hid. Instead, she asked, "Where are we going?"

Standing in a glassed cubicle, his shape appeared blurry as he turned to face her. "We are going nowhere. You will stay on the ship while I conduct business," he replied, his voice muffled.

She thought about taking offense at his high-handed manner, but curiosity prompted to ask, "What are you doing?"

"Cleansing myself, of course."

Megan craned her head from side to side as she watched lights flashing up and down his body. "How does it work? I don't hear any water."

He snorted. "We're in space, not at a resort. On board the ship, we use lasers to cleanse our bodies and rid ourselves of waste."

She wrinkled her nose. It didn't sound like much fun. "Does it hurt?"

"You tell me." Quicker than she could scream, he'd pushed open the cubicle door and yanked her in.

In the close confines of his waterless shower, she couldn't help awareness of his body—his big, naked, and virile body. She kept her eyes riveted on the goatee covering his chin. "Smooth move, but in case you hadn't noticed, I'm dressed dumbass."

"Not for long," he announced with a smirk.

"What?" She squeaked as something tickled her arm. She looked to the side and watched as the clothes she wore disintegrated into nothing. Panicked, she tried to whirl to escape, expecting to follow her garments into molecular nothingness at any moment.

Brawny arms wrapped around her and halted her escape. "Calm yourself, Earthling. The lasers won't hurt your flesh or hair. Only foreign and waste substances are evaporated."

His words of reassurance didn't stop her from pressing back against him, flesh to flesh. It also didn't stop the flare of awareness that they both were nude, and he appeared very happy to see her judging by the poking above her backside—a very thick and hard poke. To distract herself, she spoke. "Stop calling me Earthling. My name is Megan."

"Odd you should ask that seeing as how you've called me everything but my own title."

Megan bit her lip as she recalled the numerous names she'd used for him. "Fair enough, Tren."

"Thank you, Megan." He bent down to whisper her name in her ear, and she shivered. "Now turn."

"Wh-what?"

"So the lasers can get your buttocks. It won't work if you insist on plastering yourself against me. Or is this your way of saying you'd like me to copulate with you?"

"I really dislike you," she grumbled as she turned. She raised her eyes to meet his instead of lowering to see his prick, which jabbed her in the belly. She also resisted an urge to drop to her knees and see just what his giant purple Popsicle tasted like.

"Good. I'd hate to think you'll miss me when I sell you. Your new owner might take offence if you were to pine for me."

She didn't think about it. She just slugged him in the stomach and then yelled as she brought her throbbing fist to her mouth. She'd forgotten about his rock-hard body.

The jerk laughed.

Not even blinking, she brought her knee up, and connected with the underside of his cock. She enjoyed a moment's satisfaction as he shut up before she realized what she'd done. *He asked for it.* She didn't stick around to see if he agreed.

Exiting with as much dignity as she could while naked as a jaybird, she grabbed his clothes off the white counter and strode out into the bedroom to dress for the second time that morning. At least she didn't feel grimy anymore, and her bladder no longer ached. A shower and toilet in one, but without an ick factor? She grudgingly admitted the coolness of it. She patted her hair out of curiosity and discovered it didn't feel like straw anymore. Interesting. She wondered what else the shower could do.

Dressed, she bent over the table and peered at the wall he'd used the night before to feed them. Squiggles marked its surface, and she sighed as she realized she had no idea what to do.

"What are you doing?" His gravelly voice sounded right behind her, and she jumped but didn't turn to face him. Not when he was probably pissed at her knee action in the shower. *Will he spank me? Throw me onto the bed and ravish me like a pirate? Lock me in the brig?* He did nothing.

She restrained a sigh. Surely she didn't want him to lose control, or did she? "I was looking for coffee or, at the very least, something hot and imbued with caffeine."

His body bumped up into hers as he invaded her space. Her heart stuttered. "What are you doing?"

"Giving you what you asked for."

Oh god, what does he think I want? Judging by the thick cock pushing against her backside, it appeared as though he thought she needed a good hard fuck. *He might be right.*

His purple hand reached over her and…punched the wall in a sequence that lit up lights in the control panel. The hole in the wall opened, and she eyed the steaming mug with suspicion, and a little disappointment, which increased when he moved away.

Holding in another sigh, she grabbed the cup and stared at its murky contents. Did she dare drink it? "Are you mad at me?" she asked.

"No."

"Are you sure? Because I'd really hate to be poisoned because you're pissed I hurt you."

He chuckled, and the sound sent a shiver right down her spine and tickled her cleft. "You think highly of yourself if you believe your feeble blow hurt. Startled, yes, but you'd have to try a lot harder to injure me."

"Is that a dare?" She giggled when he growled. "Seriously, though, is this beverage going to screw with me like your wine did?"

"No. Now drink it and behave yourself while I conduct business."

She took a gulp of the hot liquid and swallowed happily. Nutty with a hint of bitter, it reminded her of a flavored coffee. It also bolstered her resolve. "You are not leaving me here by myself." She turned to face him as she spoke and caught him dressed only in pants, his shirt still in his hands. He turned those clear blue eyes her way, his expression too smooth for her to trust. What did he plan? Was he even now plotting how quickly he could sell her? And why did she want to cross the room and play with the silver rings piercing his chest?

"The place I am going to is not safe for females."

"But I'd be with you. Besides, what if you don't come back? I'd be stuck here and probably starve to death since I don't know how to work any of your damned buttons." She slapped the mug down on the table.

He sighed as he pulled his shirt on over his head and hid his magnificent torso. "You are truly trying my patience, Megan. There is nothing in this way station dangerous enough to keep me from coming back."

"Says you," she replied mulishly, crossing her arms over her chest.

"Yes, says me. Besides, how do you expect to join me when you have nothing to cover your feet?"

Megan looked down at her bare toes and bit her lip. Her lack of foot apparel hadn't occurred to her. "You're a pirate. Aren't you supposed to have like booty on board? Surely, you can find me a pair of shoes to wear."

Was that the sound of him gnashing his teeth? "I am not a pirate. I am an acquisitions specialist."

Megan chuckled. "You're not serious, are you?" She caught a glimpse of his austere mien and laughed harder. "Oh my god, you are. That's funny. I hate to break it to you, my giant, purple buccaneer, but on my world, the plundering of items and people without purchasing them first makes you a pirate."

"You are aggravating me again," he growled with narrowed eyes. She kind of liked it when he did that, not that she'd admit it aloud.

"What are you going to do about it? Make me walk the plank?" Megan cracked up so hard she fell onto the chair, and thus she missed him leaving, but she did catch his parting remark.

"I'll be back to pillage you later."

What should have sounded like a threat made her tingle instead. Totally unacceptable, but forewarned, she had time to prepare.

She wouldn't give in without a fight.

* * * *

Tren entered the pit station in a foul mood. Pirate indeed. *I'm not a thief. A mercenary, yes, but I don't steal.* He didn't count acquiring renewable resources from unsuspecting planets. In order for something to be counted as a theft, someone needed to notice it was gone. *And is someone missing Megan?* He told his conscious to shut up. He'd never meant to kidnap her, and as a matter of fact, if he hadn't accidentally abducted her, she would have drowned. That made him a hero, not a scurvy pirate. He'd point that fact out to her when he returned. He couldn't wait to hear her rebuttal.

While the task of refueling his ship was accomplished with ease, a lack of parts for his vessel meant he'd have to delay the repair of the thruster engine, which in turn meant another stop before he could offload Megan.

Perhaps he should invest in some ear coverings to shut out her ranting? He chuckled as he imagined her reaction, and then he caught himself. He did not find her amusing. Not in the least. With a scowl plastered to his face, he stalked through the almost deserted space station, barely noticing the sparse inhabitants that scattered from his path. A bright swath of color at a vendor's stall caught his eye, and he pivoted.

Too many credits spent later, he returned to the ship with a package tucked under one arm.

Before heading to his quarters and the feisty Earthling, he made a detour to his bridge. While setting a course for their next stop and answering communications received while he visited the barbarian galaxy, he also ensured the ship provided a meal for his captive. He wanted her well fed when he next visited her. She'd need energy for what he planned. Or hoped to have occur. Making assumptions in her case could prove erroneous, given she didn't react like any female he'd ever known. It was admittedly the most frustrating thing about her and also the most fascinating.

His work in the command room took longer than expected, but when he finally did make his way to his room, anticipation coursed through him. He refused to examine his eagerness to see her. A few times, during his tedious work, he'd thought of asking the computer to provide him a video link to his room. He'd abstained. It smacked too much of desperation, and he refused to succumb to that type of pitiful weakness.

But when he stepped into the room and discovered it in shambles, he cursed his lack of foresightedness then cursed again as something hard hit him in the head.

"What in frukx are you doing?" he bellowed.

Megan, about to swing his boot at him again, stopped and scowled. "I was trying to knock you out so I could escape this room. And it would have worked, too, if you didn't have such a bloody thick skull."

Curiosity made him ask, "And then what would you have done after you rendered me unconscious?"

She shrugged. "I don't know. Made it to your bridge and commandeered the ship I guess."

Tren tried to hold it in. Truly he did, but the laughter burst free from him and got louder the darker her look became.

"I don't see what's so funny," she muttered, crossing her arms in a way that pushed up her delectable breasts.

Tren snorted. "Firstly, you'd need something harder and require a lot more strength to subdue me with a simple blow. Secondly, my ship would never have responded to you."

"What about three?" she asked.

"There is no three. You would have never made it past the first two."

"Good to know. I'll make sure I revise my plan for next time."

She said it so seriously that Tren chuckled again. She truly had a warrior's heart in that lush body of hers. A part of him recognized he should punish her, that he at least display some sort of anger that she'd tried to hurt him and escape. Instead, he found it vastly entertaining. And besides, if she did manage to somehow slip away, he'd have hunted her down, thrown her over his shoulder and… What a shame she hadn't succeeded. Perhaps the next time he'd allow her to think she had just so he could enjoy the chase.

He tossed the package he'd carried in with him at her. She didn't catch it, even though it hit her in the stomach.

"Hey," she yelled. "What was that for?"

Tren rolled his eyes. "You were supposed to catch it."

"Did it ever occur to you to just hand it to me?"

"No. Now be quiet and open it."

"And if I refuse to shut up?"

Tren's cock swelled, and his lips curved into a partial leer. "Then I have something I can shove in your mouth to quiet you, so go right ahead."

She didn't back away or cringe in fear. On the contrary, her breathing hitched, her cheeks flushed, and her nipples hardened into points under the thin linen of his shirt. "Pig," she replied without any rancorous heat so the word sounded more like a term of endearment. "What's in the package?" she asked, changing the subject. She eyed the bundle suspiciously and shook it.

"Something you don't deserve after your antics," he retorted.

She stuck her tongue out at him and vibrated it, making a strange noise. He shook his head at her antics. Why he didn't kill her he didn't know. She aggravated him to no ends with her arguing, but he still watched her avidly as she tore open the package and pulled out its contents.

She found the shoes first, more like sandals, but she still grinned as she slid them on her feet.

"Awesome. No more freezing feet on your cold floors."

Her smile of pleasure turned to incredulity as she held up the other item he'd bought. She shook out the red gown, and Tren leaned against the wall with his arms crossed over his chest as he waited for her reaction. She didn't disappoint.

"Are you out of your fucking mind? I am soooo not wearing this—this *thing*." She sputtered with disgust, and Tren smirked.

"You requested clothing and shoes. Being a kind and generous male, I have provided items I feel will increase your worth when it comes time to sell you."

The red fabric sailed through the air to hit him in a silken flutter.

"I am not dressing in that." Her emphatic statement went well with her heaving chest and sparking eyes. It totally aroused him.

"Why ever not?" he asked in feigned innocence, provoking her further on purpose. "The material is fine silk. The color is most flattering to your complexion and will display your assets in an adequate fashion. I'll admit it wasn't easy to locate a garment to accommodate the fact you only own a single pair of breasts."

"It's a sex kitten outfit."

"A what?" He didn't understand her expression, although he could guess.

"It's smutty." He gave her a blank look, and with a huff, she continued. "It's going to make me look some walking advertisement for sex with its super short skirt and indecently low-cut neckline."

"Exactly. The perfect outfit for the auction I have planned. Unless you'd rather attend your sale naked?"

"I hate you."

"I'm a pirate, remember? I don't give a frukx what you feel."

He was ready for her when she came charging at him with her fists swinging. He'd counted on it actually. He caught her flailing fists and pulled them above her head before yanking her against his body.

"Irrational female. I buy you clothing, and this is how you repay me." He baited her, enjoying the way her cheeks flushed and her eyes flared with anger. When she opened her mouth to yell at him again, he pulled her up and kissed her.

The savage passion of their embrace ended up worth every credit he'd paid for the outfit. And then some.

Chapter Six

Megan wasn't sure how she ended up lip-locked with her purple pirate. She also didn't care after the first scorching touch.

She'd spent the day in boredom and irritation, most of it stemming from the fact he'd left her alone and, worse, horny. Every time she thought of him, her body tightened and tingled. Even as she prepared to ambush him, moisture dampened her cleft. Did a part of her know her plan wouldn't succeed? Probably, but she'd done it anyway, a perverse part of her hoping she'd goad him into touching her. Kissing her again and...

Feigning offence at the dress he'd gotten her proved easy, but not for the reason he thought. Reminding her of the fact he intended to sell her pissed her off and tempered any pleasure she might have gotten from the fact he'd not only bought her clothing but garments meant to showcase her figure. A figure he'd obviously paid attention to given he'd bought something to flatter her curves.

As she kissed him, she pressed her voluptuous frame against him, the hardness of his arousal evident against her belly, which in turn stoked her own libido. When he released her hands, she curled them around his neck and slid her fingers into the silky ends of his hair. He used his freed hands to cup her buttocks and lift her, carrying her back toward the bed. However, instead of laying her down on it, he sat and pulled her onto his lap.

Keeping her lips locked to his, she squirmed against his erection as it pressed against her bottom, enjoying his low groan. Their tongues dueled wetly, the occasional sharp edge of his teeth grazing hers and making her shudder. Hotter than she'd ever imagined getting for anyone, she mewled in loss when he pulled back from her, mollified only somewhat by his ragged breathing and the fact that his eyes were aglow with passion.

"Put the dress on," he ordered gruffly.

Amidst harsh pants of her own, she managed to mutter, "No."

"Obstinate female." A large hand clasped the back of her head, and he kissed her again fiercely while his other hand slid up her shirt and roamed the skin of her back.

Twining her own fingers into his hair, she enjoyed the luxuriant feel of the strands and the low growls he emitted when she tugged it.

Once again, he tore his mouth from hers and perused her with heavy-lidded eyes. "I told you to put it on. Obey me, Earthling."

She met his luminous gaze, her tummy swirling at the passion she could see in the depths of his eyes. Her lips curled into a taunting smile. "Make me."

Challenge thrown, he wasted no time, and she squealed as he sprang into action. In a matter of seconds, she found herself flat on her back with one of his hands on her stomach, pressing her down while the other yanked at her pants. Enjoyable as she found his manhandling—just ask her wet pussy—she didn't give in without a fight, not when the struggle excited her so. Besides, if she pretended he had to force her, then her conscience regarding abstaining from men could remain clear. Or so she told herself as she attempted to squirm and buck under his implacable grip.

She kicked and thrashed. Called him a few choice names. Clawed at him. It didn't stop him from stripping her naked—he literally tore the clothes off of her—and dressing her in the outfit best suited for a brothel, or seduction.

Once he had her clothed, he released her, and she bounded up off the bed, not far though. Whirling, she faced him and planted her hands on her hips, her bosom heaving. The brute lay back on the bed with his hands laced under his head and regarded her with a smoldering gaze. His lips curled into a grin of satisfaction. "Twirl for me."

"Screw you," she replied obstinately, cocking her hip in defiance. Her words and stance might have declared one thing, but the throbbing between her thighs and her taut nipples screamed another. *I am having way too much fun.*

"Saucy barbarian female. Can't dance? Bend over then and show me your ass. Shake it for me."

She arched a brow at him, superciliously, even as her pussy moistened and her inner channel trembled. "Seriously? I think I'll abstain. Or wait, you know what? Why don't you stand up and bend over for me? Come on, my purple marauder, strip for me and shake that thing."

The look on his face? Priceless. Her time to enjoy it? Seconds as her taunt made him bound up off the bed, his gaze intent. Stalking toward her, he stripped his shirt as he approached, revealing his delineated chest and the sexy silver rings. She swallowed hard, not in fear, but pure lust. She backed away until her ass hit the wall. She stood there, waiting, her body taut with anticipation as he approached.

"You are not very obedient," he stated, stopping a hairsbreadth from her.

Peering up at him, she licked her swollen lips. "No, I'm not. What are you going to do about it?"

"Show you who is master on this ship."

Leaning forward, he braced his hands on the wall, trapping her between his stretched arms. She stared up at him, every ounce of her tingling. Good intentions, morals, even the fact she didn't like him—or did she?—flew in the face of her desire for this pirate, this man who made her feel every inch a woman. He returned her gaze, his eyes alight in a manner she should have found freaky but, instead, fascinated her.

She expected another scorching kiss; indeed, she couldn't wait. Instead, he whirled her around so her cheek pressed against the wall and his body crowded hers from behind. Grasping her hands, he drew them above her head, holding her prisoner with only one of his by strength alone.

Oh my god, that is freaking hot.

But they still played a game, or at least she did, in order to salve her conscience. She squirmed and pulled. However, all it served to do was rub her ass against his evident erection. Not necessarily a bad thing.

His free hand curved around her waist and drew her bottom half away from the wall, arching her buttocks out. Megan's breathing hitched as he raised the skirt, baring her nude cheeks. Farther he bent her, dragging her trapped arms down as he positioned her to his liking with her ass presented to him. He leaned her over so far the pinkness of her pussy surely showed. Red stained her cheeks as he said and did nothing for a moment. A sudden fear gripped her that he would find her inadequate, too human.

"Beautiful." His murmured words sent a quiver through her, and moisture seeped from her lower lips. He traced her damp slit with his finger, a light touch that turned bolder as he delved into her channel. Megan moaned at his electric touch and then cried out as he pumped her with his digit. Rocking back against him, she drew his fingers deeper, their length enough to strike her G-spot. He stroked her over and over, building her pleasure, then his fingers left her, and she mewled with loss, a cry that turned into a short scream as he replaced the loss digits with his tongue.

Deftly, he traced her sex, slipping his tongue into her, probing her with it. He withdrew it and explored her cleft again. He found her clit, and she bucked. He grazed it again, and she jumped with a cry. The hand still manacled around her wrists gripped harder while his free hand curled around her upper thighs as an anchor. Once he'd secured her, he plied his tongue against her sensitive nub while Megan quivered, and the music of her keening joined that of his moist exploration.

The coiling tension inside her built quickly, and she didn't fight it. Her whole body tightened and then exploded. Her climax tore a loud scream from her, and still he tongued her, drawing out her pleasure.

She gasped. "Enough. I can't take anymore.

He stopped licking her. "We are far from done." A shudder rocked her channel at the promise in his words. She sensed him moving behind her and heard a rustle of fabric. A moment later, he probed her wet slit with the tip of his cock. Bent over still, Megan couldn't see him as he slid himself into her, but she could feel it, every delicious inch of him.

Thickly endowed, he stretched the walls of her sex, filling her in a satisfying way she'd never experienced before. He also finally released her hands to place both of his on her hips. Then he moved.

Slow at first, his prick slid in and out of her, the suction of her pussy gripping him tight. But he soon increased his pace, and Megan's just-sated pleasure built back. He guided the rhythm with his steady hands on her hips, drawing her into and away from his body with a speed that soon became dizzying. Even more fascinating—and enjoyable— the head of his cock seemed to expand inside her, putting pressure on her sensitive cervix and G-spot. The dual bump and rubs of her erogenous zones sent her spiraling into her second climax.

"Oh, my god!" she screamed as her second orgasm hit her harder than the first. He grunted as the walls of her sex clamped down on him tight, rippling with her bliss. His fingers dug into her soft flesh, and his body slammed one last time into hers and held itself rigid. A wet heat enveloped her womb, sending her still-shuddering climax into overdrive.

Megan almost cried at the intense pleasure of it. It wrung everything from her in an instant, leaving her boneless. He held her up, though, his strong capable hands scooping her up to carry her to bed, where he joined her, spooning her body into his. Cradled in his embrace, and with a smile on her lips, she slipped into sleep.

* * * *

Tren woke first, his body cradled against Megan's and, even worse, enjoying it. He didn't like it one bit. Females were for copulation, nothing more.

And by frukx if Megan didn't excel at that aspect. Never before had the scent and taste of woman driven him so blind with need. Even stranger, he wanted more.

His lust for her changed nothing, though. Females held no place in his life, not even one who brought forth emotions he'd never experienced previously, even one who owned an ability to make him laugh. And drive him insane.

All the more reason to sell her, and quickly. He didn't need one barbarian female messing up his existence. Although he wasn't averse to enjoying her wares until he did rid himself of her.

Now that sounded more like his usual callous self. Of course, the way he softly extricated himself from the bed so as to not wake her didn't, but he explained his gentle escape as necessary so he wouldn't have to listen to her sooner than necessary. She truly knew how to make a male wish for deafness, yet in exact reverse, he'd greatly enjoyed her cries of pleasure.

He made his way into the ablutions chamber and cleansed himself, trying to forget she slept in the room beyond. He dressed in clean clothing before exiting back into his room. He discovered her sitting cross-legged on the bed wearing his shirt, the red dress she'd fallen asleep in nowhere to be seen.

No matter, she looked fetching with her tousled hair—not as attractive as when she spilled out of the crimson gown but enough to make his prick twitch.

"Yeah, so about what happened," she said, drawing his attention from the way her breasts clung to the fabric of his shirt. "That was a mistake." His gaze narrowed. "And it can never happen again."

"Says who?" he snapped, suddenly irrationally angry. Never mind the fact he couldn't wait to get rid of her, it irritated him that she'd said it first.

"Listen, we don't like each other. Hell, you're planning on selling me to the highest bidder. As such, I think it best if we abstain from—from…" Her cheeks flushed a becoming color, and Tren's cock grew, along with his ire.

"I agree. Copulating with the merchandise is not sound business practice." He took savage pleasure in the way her mouth snapped shut and her eyes sparked with anger.

"I hate you."

For some reason her words set off something in him, and he found himself striding over to the bed. She didn't move, just watched him with wide eyes.

Hoisting her up, he stared into her face. She rendered him insane with her words. She drove him crazy with her body. She played havoc with his emotions, body, and life. But he couldn't find it in him to kill her or toss her away.

So he kissed her. And when she bit his lower lip, he bit her back.

"You are such a jerk." She panted against his mouth before proceeding to suck on his lower lip.

"And you are a noisy shrew," he rejoined as he aided her in wrapping her legs around his waist. The shirt rode up, baring her cleft. His cock found the moist entrance to her sex, and he thrust into her, enjoying her keening cry as he filled her tight channel. Hands on her buttocks, he bounced her up and down on his shaft, the tight suction of her sex tugging deliciously along his sensitized prick. Burying his face into the soft curve of her neck, he sucked on the creamy skin, taking care to not bite down—even if the urge rode him hard. To fight his irrational compulsion to claim her, he pumped her faster, and she responded by raking her nails across his upper back, a savage reaction that made him shout in pleasure. A climax roared through them both, pulsing through their bodies in blissful waves that made him collapse, almost boneless on the bed, although he took care to cradle her as they fell.

Sated and panting, face-to-face on the bed, they came to an agreement.

"I really don't like you," she began. "But for some reason, my body does. I'm sure it's only a passing thing."

"Definitely not permanent," he agreed. "But so long as we must share quarters—"

"We might as well give our bodies what they want," she finished.

They sealed their deal with a kiss and another frantic bout of copulation that left them sweaty and hungry. Of course, their eventual shower and meal rejuvenated them enough that at her frosty insistence he should clean the room and not her—because as she said with her hands planted on her hips, "I am not your bloody maid"—meant they got dirty, sweaty, and hungry all over again.

And thus did their journey—and erotic discovery of each other—last through several galactic units, Tren neglecting to stop at the planets on their path that offered entity auctions. His feeble excuse? He'd fetch a better price elsewhere. The truth? He couldn't get enough of the barbarian Earthling, and although he wouldn't admit this aloud or even contemplate it for long in his mind, he didn't want to let her go.

Accidental Abduction ~ Eve Langlais

Chapter Seven

Megan lost count of the times she fucked her purple pirate. She refused to label what they did as lovemaking, even if they cuddled afterward most times. She still lied to herself that she hated him, but her body knew the truth, even if she still remained unprepared to admit it to herself. And especially never to him.

They tried to avoid each other, him leaving to go off and do whatever he did to run the ship while she watched strange alien videos that taught her nothing other than the fact she knew absolutely nothing at all. But like yin and yang, Ben and Jerry, and every other pair who couldn't stay apart, they kept finding excuses to see each other.

Their few conversations, more like sparring matches, always ended one way—naked and panting. Actually, she did it on purpose to goad him into fucking her, but in her defense, he appeared to be doing the same thing.

For some reason, they just couldn't keep their hands off each other, even if they maintained their charade of dislike. Nor could they simply just have sex. They needed to go through a complicated dance involving shouting and manhandling—the physical wresting the part that titillated her most.

At least this time, I don't have to go through the whole betrayal thing, she mused. He made no bones about the fact that he was going to sell her as soon as he hit the right market. And yet, the funny thing was, every time she threw his plan to auction her as a sex slave in his face, he got quiet and angry. Then he always screwed her until she screamed like a banshee. Needless to say, she threw that in his face every chance she got.

They'd exchanged, in between sexual bouts and verbal battles, some bits of personal info. She'd regaled him, over another glass of that deadly wine, with all her previous failed relationships. He'd boasted of his numerous conquests. That particular conversation ended up with her throwing his sex figurines at him and calling him names, followed by raking-nails-down-his-back sex. She didn't know which of them was the more pathetic—her for continually trying and failing at love or him for avoiding it like the plague.

He still didn't trust her with his ship—wise pirate—so she found herself confined to whatever room he wanted her in. Most often the bedroom, but he did also bring her up to his bridge on occasion to give his chair a frenzied and sweaty workout.

They fell into a comfortable pattern, one that she hated to admit she enjoyed. It took her lamenting the fact that she didn't have any oils to massage his delectable body with that made her realize this was a problem. She needed distraction from the fact that she was growing feelings for her captor. Some form of the Stockholm syndrome that wouldn't end well, for her at least. Thus, when the computer announced they approached a docking station for repairs, she jumped all over it.

"I want to come with you," she declared as he clothed his magnificent body.

He didn't even bother to look at her as he replied, a shame because she'd displayed her bosom—a weak spot of his—as a distraction. "No. It's too dangerous."

"Aw, are you trying to tell me you care?" Intentionally, she baited him, and when he shot her a glare, she batted her eyelashes at him.

He growled. "You're vexing me again. You know what happens when you do that."

Megan rolled her eyes. "Well, duh. The same thing that happened, like, five minutes ago in the shower when I told you to shave because your face was roughing my girly parts up. And, like, a few hours ago in your command center chair when I declared mutiny. Now, just imagine how much I could irritate you if I came along."

His eyes flared with a look she'd come to recognize—lust. "Very well. You can come with me. But I warn you right now, if you start any trouble, I will leave you there to your fate."

A grin spread across her face as he caved in to her request. "Fine. Whatever. However, do you think while you're acting all hotshot with the locals you could find me some clothes that fit?" While his clothes were comfortable and soft, she'd prefer garments of her own. The red dress had unfortunately not survived one of their more vigorous encounters.

"Any more demands? This isn't some frukxian cruise you know," he snarled as he tugged on his boots. She ignored his attitude as she'd come to realize a few days ago it was his way of pretending he didn't like her. She knew this because she did the same thing.

"Hey, you're the one who abducted me. Now you get to deal with the consequences." She smirked at him and then chuckled at his dark glower.

She stopped laughing, though, when he strapped holsters around his waist, thighs, and arms. He proceeded to fill them with knives and pistols that he pulled out of yet another opening in the wall.

"Um, is that all really necessary?" She eyed his growing arsenal with fascination and a touch of trepidation.

He didn't bother to answer as he slid a pair of daggers into each of his boots. Armed with enough weapons for half a dozen men, he straightened and grinned, a predatory smile that displayed his pointed teeth. A sane person would have screamed, fainted, or shuddered in fear. Megan shivered all right but with lust because, by all that was holy, he looked damned good—and dangerous.

So good in fact, she delayed their departure to show him how much she liked his mercenary look.

* * * *

Tren wanted to bang his head off a wall, maybe punch a few things, and he definitely wanted to kill something. A smart male would have annihilated the female strutting along beside him, but dammit, he admired her spirit, worshiped her body, and grudgingly liked her. Even stranger, he got a feeling she liked him back. Sure, she didn't know everything about him, such as his reputation as the universe's most renowned mercenary. However, he got the feeling it wouldn't matter one whit to her. She acted like a queen—demanding and imperious.

Strangely, he enjoyed it. Enjoyed her, both in and out of bed. Not that he'd admit it out loud. *She'd use that information against me for sure*, he thought with a grin.

He still hadn't changed his mind about selling her; however, he'd decided to keep her for a longer portion of his voyage, his twisted logic dictating he'd get a better price for her nearer his home world. He also selfishly intended to enjoy as much of her naked body as he could until that time. It surprised him that he hadn't tired of her yet; actually, he still fought the urge to mark her each time she exposed her neck. Obviously, he'd caught some kind of space illness because he even looked forward to her harangues and attempts to hurt him, her feisty nature calling to something in him. Not that he let her get away with her bouts of violence and vocal displeasure. Of course his method of punishment—extreme screaming pleasure—might have had a lot to do with the fact that she didn't let up in her attempts to drive him insane.

Crazy human. My human. The possessive thought almost stopped his heart, and he must have uttered something because she peered back at him to ask, "You all right?"

Grunting in reply, he blamed his strange thought on the fact that he was taking his merchandise for a walk and would probably need to protect it. *I should add liar to my list of skills.*

Tren kept one hand on his holster as they exited the docking tunnel into the main part of the way station, a jumbled mess of buildings meshed together and covered by a dome on an asteroid circling a weak star. It was the only space station in this section of the galaxy, and one he tended to avoid because of its surcharges and ratty denizens. Given they'd sustained some minor damage during their hyperspeed flight and he still had a rear thruster in need of repair, it made sense to take advantage of the services offered here, even if the prices ranged into the obscene.

Although not as obscene as the leer thrown Megan's way by the one-eyed Kharnqiop who added to his disrespect by drooling. Tren didn't like it one bit. Stepping behind Megan, Tren bared his pointed teeth in a snarl that promised violence and extreme pain. The creature clamped its mouth shut, dropped its dozen eyes, and shuffled off, probably to spread the word he'd arrived.

Good. Teaching lessons to the hotheads who'd come crawling from the corners of this cesspit would keep him entertained while he waited for the repairs. Yet another reason he'd retired. Covert operations were harder to manage when everyone knew your face and, in an attempt to gain recognition, kept attacking—and dying. At least their feeble attempts to take him out since retirement kept him in practice. Having Megan along to protect would add an interesting element, though. *I'll kill anyone who touches her.* For business, of course. Damaged goods wouldn't fetch a nice price. He wondered how she'd feel about up close and personal violence.

Probably cheer if she thought it would benefit her.

The thought made him smirk.

He let her lead the way, which amused him since she had no idea where to go, but she faked it well with her head held high, stalking like she owned the place. Spilling out into the main thoroughfare, crowded with beings from a multitude of races, she finally halted. He moved to stand beside her, his presence claiming her without words as his property.

He let her look around with wide eyes before he nudged her in the direction they needed to go. "Stop gawking. You look like fresh meat."

"Well, excuse me for suffering some culture shock. It's one thing to meet you, you kind of look human. But this…" She inclined her head. "That's freaking wild."

Tren tried to view it for a moment from her perspective, the scene before them one he'd seen a hundred times before. Beings of all shapes, sizes, colors, and in possession of appendages in the single to double digits roamed the marketplace. Normal stuff. He shrugged. "You'll get used to it. Now come on. We need to get the work order in before the first ones arrive."

"First what?"

Tren didn't bother answering. He just took off at a brisk walk, and after a moment's hesitation, she followed. But, of course, she didn't walk behind him in a position of subservience. She placed herself on his left and, with her lips tight, pretended an aloofness he could tell by her tight body she didn't feel. Frukx, but he admired her spirit.

Locating the grungy office of the service station, he sauntered in and slammed his fist down on the counter. A familiar face appeared as the mechanic came scurrying in from the back. Tren sneered as the creature blanched. He relayed his instructions on repair to the three-armed mechanic, who bobbed his head in deference. Tren made sure to keep one eye on Megan, who prowled around with way too much curiosity in her eyes. She also looked much too enticing in his oversized shirt, the sway of her breasts entirely too visible.

Tren growled, and the mechanic stepped back, swallowing hard with all five of his mouths. He fixed his gaze on the creature. "I expect it done within one astral unit."

"But the other clients—"

Tren leaned forward and grabbed the mechanic by the neck. "Do you need to lose another arm?" Annoyed at the exorbitant rates they'd charged him last time, and the scratch they'd put on his hull, Tren had displayed his displeasure in a way that left a permanent impression.

Frantic head bobbing answered him, and Tren released the alien, a sudden prickling on the back of his nape making him whirl. Megan no longer lurked the shop, having stepped out into the thoroughfare.

And of course, she'd found trouble.

Chapter Eight

"Unhand me right now," Megan demanded, hiding her fear behind false bravado. Not an easy task considering the slimy grasp of the blue octopus holding her wrist.

A gurgle she suspected passed as a chuckle made her grimace. "That was totally gross. And I said let me go." When the alien creature ignored her and started tugging, her sandaled feet sliding, she got mad.

"You must be a male under all that disgusting goo." She pulled out a chopstick saved from one of their dinners. After seeing Tren's own preparations, she'd tucked it into her pants in case of an emergency. This certainly counted. She jabbed the oversized needle into the tentacle holding her. The icky alien squealed as it released her. Megan took a step back and bared her teeth in a grimace as she waved her makeshift rapier at it.

Its eyes, all half dozen of them, fixated on something behind her. It shrieked again, even louder, as a big, familiar body rushed past her. Tren picked up the extraterrestrial as if it weighed no more than a feather and threw it against a corrugated wall. It hadn't even begun sliding down, leaving a slimy trail, when Tren pulled out a pistol and fired.

A great big hole appeared in the middle of the creature while Megan watched with her jaw dropped low enough to hit her toes. Given she could have stuck her hand through the octopus thingy without touching its insides, she presumed it was dead.

Tren holstered his gun and turned to face her. The dangerous glitter in his eyes and the tenseness of his face sent a jolt of pure desire through her. *Oh my god, I think that was the single most, hottest thing any man has ever done for me.* She ignored the fact that she'd just about saved herself before he'd arrived. She admired the way he took charge and protected her.

"You are uninjured?" he asked, his clear blue eyes checking her up and down.

"Slimed, but fine. You know, I'd just about taken care of him," she announced as she held up her chopstick.

A smile tugged his lips. "Yes, you did. I just made an example of him to warn others away. You are not upset I killed it?"

She shrugged. "I might have felt different if it were a human you just shot a cannon through, but I never did care for seafood."

He snorted, tried to stop it, but couldn't. He laughed aloud, a mirthful sound that proved contagious, and she joined him. She vaguely noticed that some of the alien folks walking by stopped to gape at them, but she paid them no mind. Tren owned the most awesome laugh, and she got the impression he didn't use it often. It pleased her to know she'd caused it, even if unintentionally.

"Stow your vicious weapon, my feisty barbarian. We wouldn't want to frighten the shop owners into closing before we can purchase some items."

Megan tucked the chopstick into her waistband before sauntering off. "Shopping. Cool.

Think we can find some more shoes? I'd love to find some steel-toed combat boots in my size. These sandals suck for kicking balls with."

Tren snorted, and Megan grinned as she perused the storefronts that made her think of home. Well, if you discounted the fact that the garments on display owned several sleeves and the shopkeepers all resembled mad science experiments.

Adrenaline from the fight wore off, and she hid an internal quiver as she pretended interest in the wares offered by creatures straight out of *Men in Black*. Her mind whirled as it finally hit her. She'd not only stabbed something living, but she'd also watched it get killed for just touching her. While she didn't regret her actions—and still found his hot—it made her wonder exactly how violent she could expect her new life to end up. Judging by the occasional grunts and thumps that she heard from behind her where Tren followed, probably often.

A savage part of her approached the concept with glee. No more false politeness or putting up with bullshit. But then again, as with all things, only the strongest would prevail. Currently, Tren protected her, but what about when he relinquished ownership of her—not something she wanted to truly think of, but she'd always been a realist. What skills did she have to survive other than an acerbic tongue? In a battle of fists or weapons, speech wouldn't gain her a thing.

In sudden inspiration, she whirled to speak to Tren and almost bit her tongue, trying to hold in laughter. She found him with one fist cocked while his other hand held up a goblin-like creature by the neck. He appeared sheepish at having gotten caught.

"Don't mind me. Finish what you were doing." She waved magnanimously.

Flashing a savage grin, Tren turned back to his blanching victim. A few smacks and a toss later, he swiveled back to face her. Megan shook her head at him as she took in the devastation that seemed to follow in their wake. "Does this happen to you often?"

He shrugged. "More or less. I told you to stay on the ship."

"I didn't say I minded. It does, however, explain your arsenal, and it is part of what I wanted to talk to you about. I wanted to know if you'd teach me how to protect myself. I'm starting to realize I can't count on cops and laws to really protect me out here."

"I will protect you," he growled, his gaze narrowing in displeasure.

"For now. But what about once you sell me? You won't be around. " His face darkened, but she forged on. "So, please, would you teach me something so I'm not so helpless?"

"You are far from helpless," he barked as he strode away.

She hurried to catch him. "Oh, come on. You and I both know I wouldn't stand a chance against a real badass."

He stopped suddenly and whirled. "A real what?"

"You know a thug. Bad guy. Vicious killer. I'd be toast in a second." She drew a finger across her throat and made a choking sound.

He snorted. "I don't think you have much to fear. You've stood your ground fairly well against me."

Megan rolled her eyes. "Now I know you're placating me. You don't count. I mean, you might be a pirate and all, but that doesn't make you a bad guy. I'm talking about super mean, cold-hearted dicks. The kind who would hurt me in a heartbeat."

Tren choked. "You don't consider me a danger?"

"Well, duh. You're a nice guy for a buccaneer. I mean, sure, you're big and annoying, but you've never actually done anything to hurt me."

"And what about this?" he asked, splaying his arm to showcase the limping forms, and, in some cases, corpses, that littered their path.

She snorted. "We're in a den of iniquity. Attacks are to be expected. Self-defense is not a crime, so don't feel bad."

Her words made his face twist from disbelief to humor to smoking intensity. A hand shot out, and he grabbed a hold of her, yanking her toward him until she reeled against his chest. "Silly female. Don't you realize I am the most dangerous thing you will encounter?" he whispered before hoisting her up for a kiss that stole her breath.

Megan forgot they stood in the middle of an alien marketplace. Forgot the violence trailing them. Forgot even her own name as his lips slanted over hers in a possessive embrace that turned her knees to jelly and sent moist heat to pool in her cleft. She curled her arms around his neck and tugged him closer. Sliding her tongue between his lips, she shuddered as he sucked it and then grazed it with his teeth.

Kissing him just never grew old. No matter how many times they touched she could never get enough. Arousal flushed her body and made her wish for a more intimate setting, especially when a sarcastic voice intruded.

"Well, well. Isn't this cozy?"

* * * *

Tren kept one arm wrapped around Megan as he pulled and aimed a pistol at the only other male in the universe who could hope to sneak up on him. His damned brother, who also doubled as his worst enemy.

The cold gaze of his only sibling didn't flinch, even though Tren kept his gun level with his smirk.

"What do you want, Jaro?" Tren's voice came out low and tight. Megan, for once, said nothing, but she did turn in his grasp, her back plastered to his front. He bit back a grin as he felt her hand move to grip the end of the eating prong. She certainly didn't lack courage.

"Want? Does a brother need a reason to exchange pleasantries? It's been a long time, Tren. Forgive me if I find myself curious as to how you've been."

"I am fine. Now leave and get on with your business." Tren muttered the words through gritted teeth. Jaro just smiled at him coolly.

"Do you always hold family members hostage?" Megan's voice pierced their impasse, and he held back a groan as she drew Jaro's attention.

"And who might you be?" Jaro asked with a sneer.

"On Earth, I'm called Megan, but according to Tren, I'm probably known as a new pair of shoes. Or maybe a shirt depending on the price he can get for me when he sells me. Apparently, I'm annoying, so I might not fetch a good price."

Her outspoken declaration, which Jaro unfortunately understood given he also wore a translator, was almost worth the dropped jaw and wide eyes on his brother. But it didn't last, and Jaro's gaze quickly narrowed. "I didn't know you'd taken to slave trading, brother."

Tren would have answered with a scathing remark, but Megan was on a roll.

"Oh, he didn't intend to. He accidentally abducted me when he was fishing on my planet. See, my boyfriend decided to kill me and tossed me into the ocean. Lucky me, I got kidnapped by a pirate, and now I get to look forward to being auctioned off as a sex slave, or an appetizer, depending, I guess, on the buyer's taste."

"Megan!" Tren growled her name, and she turned in his arms to smile up at him with false innocence.

"What? Did I say something wrong?" With a smirk, she turned back to face his nemesis.

"Nothing wrong at all, dear Megan," Jaro interjected smoothly, drawing her attention. "I apologize for my brother. Personally, had I discovered a gem like yourself in my hold, I would have dressed you in fine fabrics and wooed you as obviously befits someone of your beauty."

Tren growled. He couldn't help himself as his brother flirted with Megan, and she seemed to soak it up, even though the touch of his kiss surely still lingered on her lips. It angered him, rousing a possessive jealousy he'd never known before.

Megan tittered, and Tren gritted his teeth. *Surely, she doesn't fall for his flowery lies?*

"What a load of crap," Megan crowed. Her laughter turned derisive, and Tren watched in satisfaction as Jaro's face tightened in anger. "You didn't seriously think I'd believe that load of drivel, did you?" She snorted. "I might be considered a barbarian, but even I'm not that gullible."

"You should watch your tongue, else you might find yourself without it," Jaro growled.

Tren didn't like his menacing tone, but apparently Megan liked it even less. In what he was coming to realize was her signature move, she kneed his brother between the legs. As Jaro gasped, she smiled at him sweetly. "That's for being a dick to your brother. And this…" She kneed Jaro again in the stomach. "Is for being an asshole in general." Megan turned to face Tren and stood on tiptoe to brush her lips over his. "I'll see you back on the ship for my *punishment*," she announced with a wink. She pulled away from him and made her way back to their vessel, her buttocks wiggling enticingly. Tren tracked her passage while his brother straightened with a wheeze.

"I will kill—"

Jaro never finished his sentence because Tren grabbed him around the throat and slammed him up against a wall. "I wouldn't finish that sentence if I were you, else I might just forget the promise made to our mother and end you right now."

Jaro's eyes widened, incredulity blatant in his expression. "Don't tell me you care for that crass, barbaric female?"

"Of course not," Tren scoffed. "She is a female, and one slated for sale once I find the right market for her."

"I look forward to bidding on her then. I think she'd look splendid spread-eagle on my bed—naked. She won't be able to say much with my cock stuffed down her throat."

"Oh no, you won't." A jealous rage gripped him. Tren knew it was foolish, even as he drew his fist back and knocked his brother out. In that one act, he'd let his sibling know Megan meant more to him than he let on. More than he even wanted to admit to himself.

Looking at his brother's slumped form, a part of Tren regretted the past that had brought them both to this point. But a man could only apologize so many times. It was time Jaro got over it.

Tren banged on the counter of the hiding shopkeeper who peered at him with frightened eyes. "You recognize me I assume?" The peeking head nodded. "Good. I expect you to ensure he comes to no harm, or I'll come back and show you in violent detail why you don't piss me off." Tren turned to walk away but stopped and pivoted back. "Oh, but feel free to compensate yourself for the trouble by taking anything he has on him."

Tren chuckled as he imagined Jaro's reaction when he regained consciousness, nude as the day of his birth. He might have promised his mother he wouldn't kill his brother, but he'd never said anything about humiliation.

Concerned that Megan might have encountered trouble on her way back to the ship—or caused it—he stepped over Jaro's prone form and headed in her direction.

He discovered only one miscreant in need of dispatching on his way, his guilt evidenced by the silver prong pinning his hand to the wall beside the opening leading to his ship. He dispatched him quickly and stalked in after her, angry even if he didn't understand why.

Chapter Nine

Megan paced in front of the opening for the ship, unable to get in no matter how much she whacked the wall but unwilling to go back out looking for Tren. It didn't help she'd left her only weapon stuck in some alien who'd grabbed her ass.

What unsettled her wasn't her sudden propensity for violence or the odd encounter with his brother, but the scalding kiss. The one he'd given her in public and with that strange look in his eye. A brain-muddling, knee-melting, panty-wetting kiss. He'd embraced her and she forgotten everything except how it felt to be in his arms. She wondered if she would have even protested had he decided to take her in full view of everyone. Probably not, given how hot her blood ran. The thought chilled her, but not as much as what she feared it meant.

I don't even like him. Sure, he's sexy, but dammit, the guy wants to sell me as some sex toy for some pervert. Yet, even knowing this, she enjoyed his presence and craved his touch. Once again, like an idiot, she was allowing herself to trust a man, care for him even though all signs pointed to him eventually hurting her. And she'd only have herself to blame. He'd made his intentions clear from the start. She was the stupid one for allowing her heart to get involved. She blamed it on her body and its insane desire for him. If only she could slake her never-ending thirst where he was concerned.

Speaking of the purple devil, he arrived, striding up the gangway, his brows arched and his lips pulled into a taut line. "Why are you standing outside the ship?" he barked.

"Probably because I don't know how to get in."

"It wouldn't have mattered if you did. My ship only responds to my touch." He slapped the panel beside her head, and the door slid open.

"Then why bother to ask why I'm standing here?"

"To irritate you," he replied with an unrepentant grin.

Instead of blasting him, she turned and gave him her rear. About to walk in, she stopped as he halted her. "Aren't you forgetting something?"

She whirled back and then bit her lip as he handed her back the chopstick she'd left behind. "Thanks."

His lips quirked. "I'd say no trouble, but I'd say that follows you wherever you go."

She shrugged. "What can I say? I'm gifted." She spun away from him and headed into the ship.

"Megan." He spoke her name softly, and again she stopped to peer back. She couldn't read the look in his clear eyes, and his brow furrowed. "I will be back shortly. Try and stay out of mischief." For some reason, she got the impression he'd meant to say something else.

Nodding in reply, she didn't let her shoulders slump until the door slid shut.

What had she expected? That he would suddenly sweep her into his arms and resume the kiss from earlier? The one that seemed to speak of more than passion, but... No, she wouldn't even think it. From now on, it was probably best if they stayed away from each other. Far away.

Common sense didn't stop the disappointment, though.

It took her several slap attempts along the corridor wall, but she finally made it to the command center. She sat in the chair and twirled her hair as she waited for him to return.

"Hey, computer, I don't suppose you've got any new videos to watch?" she muttered aloud.

To her surprise, the view screen lit up, and she leaned forward with rapt attention as she found herself treated to real-time footage of the marketplace she'd just left.

From her position of safety, she studied the various races milling about, all the while waiting to catch sight of her purple marauder. It took a while, during which she watched an almost comical display of violence amongst the various alien species, but Tren finally appeared, stepping forth from a building, from which hung a bright red, flashing sign that she couldn't read.

Annoyance made her flush and drum her fingers as she guessed what it said, given he had some alien females hanging off each arm. Their numerous breasts pressed against him, and he, the freaking jerk, did nothing to push them away. On the contrary, he smiled and patted the hand of one.

Fuming, she crossed her arms and turned sideways in the chair to avoid seeing him bestowing anything more intimate on the hussies. Irrational jealousy ate at her. She didn't own him and had no say in whom he spent his time with, and apparently, no matter how many times they'd fucked, the first chance he got, he preferred paying for it, which said a lot about her skill— or lack of.

She didn't care. *He's a slaving pirate who intends to auction me off,* and if he thought he'd get any more tastes of the goods, he had another thing coming.

When he finally arrived in the command center, she wouldn't swivel to face him.

"I see you finally managed to figure out some of the ship commands," he announced.

"With no help from you," she grumbled.

"I was otherwise occupied," he retorted.

"Yes, I saw how you were *busy*," she drawled with thick sarcasm. She pivoted in the seat and fixed him with a sneer.

"Are we back to acting irrational?" he snapped back.

She arched a brow. "Me? I never realized I'd stopped. And don't try to change the subject. I'm not the one who can't make up his mind."

Tren gaped at her. "What the frukx are you yammering about now?"

"Don't act so innocent. I saw you with those-those things."

His gaze flicked to the view screen, which still ran the live footage of the market place. His brow cleared in understanding. "I admit, I didn't know what would please you, hence my difficulty in choosing."

"Please me?" She jumped up from the chair and stalked toward him. She poked him hard in the chest and then poked him again just because she enjoyed it. "Just because I let you fuck me doesn't mean I'm open to your sick sexual fantasies."

Tren stared at her with incomprehension. "How did we get back to sex? My errand was one of your asking. Or did you change your mind about acquiring a new set of clothing and shoes?"

"Clothing?" Megan's brow wrinkled. "What's clothing got to do with those sluts groping you?"

Comprehension dawned on him, and he laughed. "You saw me with the seamstresses and thought I spoke of bringing them back for a group orgy?" Megan blushed, and he chuckled louder.

Annoyed at her mistake, she slugged him in the groin and then stomped on his foot for good measure. It didn't stop his laughter or his arms from coming around her frame to tug her into him for a bone-crushing hug.

"This isn't funny," she muttered, her cheeks hot with embarrassment.

"I find your jealousy highly entertaining." He rubbed his chin across the top of her head, and his gentle gesture made it hard for her to hold on to her irritation.

"I am not jealous. I'd have to like you for that emotion to work." But his words slapped her in the face with the truth. *Fucking hell, if I'm jealous, then I must like him.*

"Liar," he chided.

Yes, she was, and she didn't like what it implied. Not enjoying where this conversation headed both aloud and in her mind, she changed the subject. "So, what's up between you and your brother? I see he got both the looks and the charm. Is that why you don't get along?" Her jibe stifled his humor, and he stepped away from her, taking his masculine warmth with him, and, for a moment, she regretted her words.

"My argument with my brother is none of your concern. And in the future, if you should encounter him again, you would do well to watch yourself. I might be renowned in the galaxy, but he is the scourge of it."

"Nice family," she sassed. "I think I'll skip the family reunion if you don't mind. Somehow it doesn't seem like a safe affair."

"I have no family, well, other than Jaro, and we don't run into each other often."

Megan bit her lip. "I'm sorry. I didn't know." It would explain why he'd never spoken of his upbringing.

Tren shrugged, his face expressionless. "My father died when my brother and I were still young. A failed mission. My mother succumbed to an injury over ten planetary cycles ago."

"You still have your brother, though, even if you don't currently get along."

"Only because we promised our mother not to kill each other," he growled, pacing the bridge.

"Maybe you can patch things up." It bothered her to see him so agitated and to discover he was just as alone in the universe as she was.

"Enough. I will not speak of this further." He held up a hand to forestall any further commentary on her part.

The computer's voice interrupted them. "Incoming message from the Galactic Council."

Tren's brows drew together. "What in frukx do they want? They know I am retired."

"Who's the Galactic Council?" Megan asked. "And what did you retire from?"

"None of your affair. You'll have to leave so I can hear the message. I've left the package with your new garments in my quarters."

Megan knew a brushoff when she heard it. It still annoyed her. She'd begun to walk toward the elevator when he caught her and spun her around. Drawing her up on tiptoe, he kissed her, a hard bruising embrace that stole her breath.

She didn't say anything when he let her down, just stared at his eyes, which glowed with intensity. "I will be along shortly. I expect to see you wearing something new. Or else," he warned with a wink.

Megan blew him a raspberry in reply, which made him chuckle. Smiling herself, she left him, entering the elevator that would take her back to his quarters. As she exited into the corridor, a tremor rocked the ship, and Megan braced her hand against the wall.

What the fuck was that?

An alarm sounded, which didn't reassure her but the sound was not as bad as the frisson of fear that struck her when the lights went out.

Megan froze, surrounded by pitch-black. Somehow she doubted this boded well, a belief that tripled when she heard a scuffling sound echoing somewhere in the corridor with her.

"Tren?" She hated the quaver in her voice. However, she forgave herself in this instance. Seriously, the situation warranted it.

Nobody replied, but the skin on her nape prickled, announcing the fact that she shared the dark hall with someone—or something—else. She reached at her waist for her needle, only to curse silently as her hand didn't locate it. She'd left it in the bridge during her wait for Tren.

A whisper of sound from behind made her whirl, not that she could see anything. She punched forward with her fists and was rewarded with contact and a grunt, but her feeble blow didn't stop the fabric from getting pulled over her head or the prick in her arm.

"Tren's going to fucking kill you for touching his merchandise," she slurred to her unseen attacker before slumping to the floor unconscious.

Chapter Ten

Tren stood for a moment watching the elevator door, wishing he could follow Megan instead of wasting time listening to a message he had no interest in.

But I will not chase after a female. Brave words that made him sigh and his cock sulk. "Play the message from the council," he ordered aloud to the computer.

He'd no sooner settled into his chair than the screen lit up with the Galactic Council crest, but the face that appeared immediately after had him jumping from his seat and growling.

"Z'nistakn, what the frukx do you want?"

The green-scaled humanoid flicked a forked tongue and chuckled, a gravelly, wet sound. "I want what I always have, your head on a platter and your entrails on my plate."

Tren smiled coldly. "Threats? Are you really so stupid? I could use a new pair of boots."

The councilor hissed, and his slitted yellow eyes narrowed. "First, you'd have to find me, filthy mercenary."

"Don't tempt me," he replied, not letting on that he already knew the location of the corrupt councilor's supposed safe base. Tren wondered what Z'nistakn was truly after. Idle chitchat didn't seem like his usual style.

"I have a job for you."

And now they got to the true point of the call. "I'm retired."

"Surely you could make an exception. I would make it worth your while." The reptile drummed his clawed fingers on his armrest.

Tren wanted to reach through the view screen and throttle the creature. He'd disliked the dishonest galactic councilor for quite some time, a feeling reciprocated, and yet Z'nistakn still called upon his services, even though Tren kept declining. "I'm busy."

"So I've heard. Cavorting with a human female. I thought you enjoyed better taste."

Tren restrained himself from growling. What did he care if the slimy councilor insulted Megan? She simply satisfied a need. "Find another mercenary to do your dirty work. I'm not interested."

The councilor's forked tongue flicked out again, and he sighed with exaggeration. "Well, I am glad to hear it isn't the barbarian female making you soft. In that case, you won't miss her."

Before Tren could retort, an explosion jarred his ship, and Z'nistakn chortled. Tren cut the communication and moved, even as his computer warned him.

"Rear hatch blown. Unauthorized life forms boarding. Sealing—"

An invisible pulse made the air around him waver and sent a shiver through his body. The voice of the machine abruptly cut off as the power supply to his vessel died and pitched him into darkness. Very little could incapacitate his vessel, but the well-aimed electromagnetic pulse would temporarily throw everything offline. His whole system would reboot with an astral quarter unit.

"Frukx!" Tren cursed aloud but didn't remain still. He needed to get to Megan. The dark didn't bother him. He'd long ago gotten the visual enhancements that allowed him to see better than most nocturnal creatures. He also wouldn't let a paltry thing, such as a lack of power, keep him from Megan. *Not when she needs me.*

As he pried up the hatch in the elevator floor, he called himself all kinds of names for stopping at this way station and not remaining more on guard. Usually nobody or anything could get close enough to his ship to do damage, but he'd allowed the repair crew to do so and without supervision. Under normal circumstances, he oversaw all adjustments; however, this time, he'd found himself preoccupied with one feisty female. A lesson learned that he wouldn't repeat.

In the meantime, he needed to rectify his error, and quickly. Megan faced danger, alone.

Unacceptable.

Tren slid down the laddered rungs in the elevator shaft, mentally counting until he reached the correct floor. He pried the doors open and dove into the corridor, ducking into a roll as he drew his guns. He ended up on one knee with both his arms extended, his guns primed to fire.

However, of Megan, he saw nothing. Going on instinct, he bypassed his quarters and ran for the other end of the corridor where the lesser-used secondary elevator shaft resided. The gaping maw of its opening made him run faster, and he flew down the ladder. He navigated the warren of tunnels and utility shafts on the lowest level, easily locating the blown hatch the attackers used to force their way in. He ducked through the ragged opening and emerged into the work bubble erected around the lower thruster section as the garage performed repairs.

Peering around, Tren's jaw tightened at the realization Megan was gone. Anger battled with sinking dread.

A smart acquisitions specialist would have let her go, chalked her up as a loss, one barbarian female's worth not equal to the damage or fuel expense of a chase and recapture. An intelligent male would have looked upon the situation as the easiest method in which to rid himself of a copulation partner without fear of reprisal.

But Megan belonged to him. *And no one takes what is mine.*

* * * *

Megan woke to a thick tongue and a pounding head. She blinked her eyes open and didn't like what she saw, so she closed them. She took a deep breath then another. All in all, she took about ten shuddering breaths before she opened her eyes again.

Nope, still a bad situation. *Damn.*

Kind of like her first abduction, she found herself unable to move; however, unlike the last time, she found herself shackled against a wall.

Kidnapped, but not by a nice purple pirate this time if I'm not mistaken.

She wondered if Tren even knew they'd taken her yet. If he cared. Probably not, given how much trouble he claimed she continually was. Perhaps he'd see her kidnapping as a relief. Sure, he'd miss out on a bit of profit, but now he didn't have to put up with her.

Megan gave her head a shake. Enough with the pity party. He'd never claimed to care for her, and it wasn't as if she cared for him. He just happened to provide great sex—and a cuddly body to sleep entwined with. And…

She growled as her mind tried to smash through her defenses. She fought back. She couldn't allow herself to care for him—or trust him. Therein lay the path to stupidity and heartache. Besides, she had more important items to worry about, such as how to escape her untenable situation.

A yank at the manacles holding her proved useless. The noise, however, created a scuffle outside the cell door.

The heavy portal-like door swung open, and the three-armed mechanic from the space station sauntered in.

"It took you long enough to wake," he complained, and Megan watched in fascination as his five mouths moved at different speeds. It made her wonder what she would have heard if she didn't wear a translator. She hoped the damned alien was wearing a translator of his own because she didn't want to waste the insults her mind prepared otherwise.

"Well, excuse me, you three-armed freak, for succumbing to your kidnapping drug so thoroughly. Next time, give me a bit of warning before you decide to abduct me and I'll try to build a resistance to it first." She spoke without thinking, a never-ending fault with her no matter the situation.

"Where we're taking you there won't be a second chance." The creature chuckled, pleased with his threat and answering the question that, yes, he could understand her. Perfect, time to put her most effective weapon to use—her acerbic tongue and attitude.

Megan sighed. "You know, I really wish you bad guys would come up with something original. Do you know how many times that phrase has been done in the movies? Seriously. Would it kill you to come up with something new? And maybe take a shower? I mean, seriously, you've definitely got something funky going on."

"You talk too much," said the alien with a frown, three of his five mouths pulling down in a moue of displeasure.

"So everybody tells me. What are you going to do about it?"

He slapped her in the face, which really hurt but also fired up Megan's temper. "Oh, big bad alien. Hit a defenseless woman, why don't you? Coward. What's wrong? Afraid if I wasn't tied up I'd hurt you?"

The mechanic-turned-kidnapper snarled. "Filthy-mouthed whore."

"Not for you I won't be. I like my men with some balls. I think you left yours at home. Or did someone already neuter you?" Megan's smile goaded him as much as her provoking words.

That time, when he punched her, she tasted blood, but he still didn't give in to her taunts and unchain her. A pity. She'd hoped to shame him into doing so.

Worse, the sight of her blood excited him, and he began to rain blows on her body, leaving no part of her undamaged. Through the haze of pain and blood, she could hear him talking to himself.

"Take off my arm and beat me with it, will you? Ha. Looks like I get the last laugh. I've got your woman now, Trenkaluan. Not such a tough mercenary after all. And once I'm done showing this whore her place, I'm going to let her service me. How do you like that, you smug bastard?"

"You're nuts," she muttered. "Tren doesn't care for me."

"Liar," spat the alien, his mouths contorting out of sequence. "He's never been seen with a woman outside of a brothel before. You must mean something, and I am going to ruin you for him. Sully you and then throw it in his face. And he won't be able to do a thing about it."

"That's what you think," growled a surprising, but welcome, voice.

He came for me!

Chapter Eleven

Tren cursed the time it took to get his ship back online and discard the repair bubble. He used those wasted moments to imagine how he'd torture the three-armed bastard who'd dared move so brazenly against him.

Of course, he had only his distraction for one female to blame for getting caught off guard. Then again, if the cowards had come for him, he'd have taken care of the problem, distraction or not, but they'd instead dared to go after Megan. Just the thought of her in someone else's grasp made his anger burn hotter than a star gone super nova.

Locating them proved easy once he got on his way. Megan's translator also contained a tracking device, an expensive upgrade he'd acquired for a project he'd ended up passing on a while back. His ship followed the blip of her signal while he armed himself and prepared to unleash a miniature war.

Nobody frukxed with him and lived to tell the tale.

When he got within radar range, he engaged the cloaking device. Another expensive toy, but a lack of wealth had stopped being a barrier a long time ago. His larger craft shadowed the vessel holding Megan. He made his way to the lowest deck, not the section where the dead-aliens-walking had entered, but another smaller section especially built for space embarkations. Fingers flying on the console, he engaged his boarding mechanism, which lowered a metal tube. It connected to the other vessel's surface with only the slightest thud.

Tren braced his feet over the hatch as it hissed open and dropped through as soon as it was clear. He hit the surface of the other vessel and went to work with a laser cutting through the metal. As soon as the piece dropped, providing him entry, he followed, his knives pulled. In space, only the insane used guns, which could punch holes into vital areas. Usually, he was that crazy person, but he needed to ensure Megan's safety before he let loose.

The storage room he entered, while loaded with stolen goods, did not contain anything for him to kill. A shame.

A scan of the ship by his own computer showed only six life forms on board—Megan plus five idiots. A paltry amount. The first two he found in the bridge, oblivious to the vessel anchored above them. They managed to turn only halfway to greet him when he slit their throats before they could raise an alarm. Wiping his blades on their carcasses, he moved quickly to search room by room. The crewman exiting from a stateroom managed a squeal before Tren thrust his dagger into him and dragged it up, eviscerating him.

Cold rage drove him as he methodically hunted the remaining two. He located the fourth miscreant standing outside an open doorway, watching something eagerly. Tren could hear a voice muttering and the fleshy smacks of someone getting beaten. Tren ran at the inattentive guard and thrust both daggers into its back, using them to lift and move the gurgling thug out of his way.

Tren stood framed in the doorway, and his fury coalesced from angry red to an icy white. The three-armed mechanic, who should have known better than to frukx with him, slugged Megan, who hung bruised and bloody from a set of manacles.

He caught the soon-to-be-dead alien midsentence. "…like that, you smug bastard?"

"You're nuts," she muttered. "Tren doesn't care for me." Her words struck him like a blow.

"Liar," spat the alien. "He's never been seen with a woman outside of a brothel before. You must mean something, and I am going to ruin you for him. Sully you and then throw it in his face. And he won't be able to do a thing about it."

"That's what you think," Tren growled, more angry than he recalled ever being. He didn't need his knives for this, so he sheathed them as he flowed into the room, vengeance personified.

The mechanic snarled as he drew a knife of his own and lunged at him. Tren didn't move. He caught the flailing wrist and the second, which came out of nowhere with another blade. He yanked and twisted the appendages as the third hand came thrusting at him—and missed. The crack and snap as bone broke preceded the wailing scream of the alien. But Tren wasn't done. He grabbed the third arm and snapped it, too.

The idiot, who'd thought to best him, collapsed screaming. The noise irritated Tren, so he kicked it in the head, knocking it unconscious.

Then he turned to face his human.

Megan, even with all her injuries, retained enough wits to gape at him. "You actually came for me?"

He shrugged. "Did I mention I hate pirates?"

She laughed, a sound tinged with pained hysteria. "You're insane."

"Probably. But I wouldn't talk if I were you. What did I tell you about trouble?" He spoke to her gently, trying to keep her attention on him as he used his knives to pry open the manacles. The left one popped open, and he went to work on the other.

"I know. I just keep making that profit margin of yours smaller and smaller."

"If this keeps up, I might have to keep you for a while until you work off some of your debt."

The restraint snapped off, and she collapsed against him. He caught her with one arm, hugging her tight to him, his rage burning anew at her weakness and injury.

"I'm sorry I'm such a pain in the ass," she whispered against his chest. "You should have left me to die."

"Never," he almost yelled, the very thought of her death chilling him through and through. But she never heard his reply as she slipped into unconsciousness.

A myriad of feelings swirled in him. He wanted to wake her up and shake her for allowing herself to succumb to despair. He wanted to crush her tight to him and keep her forever safe. He wanted to kiss her until she smiled. He wanted to weep with relief that he'd found her.

I've truly lost my mind, and he was no longer sure he cared, a situation he'd examine later. Right now, Megan needed tending.

He swung her up into his arms and headed back out into the main hall. Reaching his created entrance, he held onto her with one arm as he used his other to grasp a hanging harness that his ship dropped at his command. The crank, holding the suspended cable, hoisted him and his precious burden up. He wouldn't—couldn't—let her go as he tapped in the commands to separate his vessel from the now-vacant one. The hatch closed with a metallic click, and Tren heard the sound of the metal tube retracting. He didn't bother calling up a view screen to watch the fireworks when he ordered his computer to fire on the other vessel as soon as they were at a safe range.

More important matters called to him, such as getting Megan to the medical unit as quickly as possible. He laid her on the table with care, stripping her bloodied garments, a strange moisture in his eyes as he visually catalogued her external hurts. A low moan emerged from him when he read the list of internal injuries she'd suffered because he'd failed her in the first place. In that moment, he vowed to never let her down again. To never allow another to hurt her.

And I'm never letting you go.

* * * *

Megan's eyes fluttered open and, worried about what she saw, she shut them quickly.

Oh no, I died.

She tried to calm her breathing, which quickened as she took stock of her situation. The last thing she remembered was collapsing in Tren's arms as he rescued her, the screaming pain of her body making her faint. That agony seemed gone, which given Tren's alien technology, seemed possible. But the soft surface she found herself on, a fluffy cloud, for sure, and the frescoed ceiling above her certainly didn't resemble either his ship or anything else she'd ever encountered in her life.

Hence, she must have died and gone to some alien heaven.

That sucked. *I'll miss my damned pirate.*

A tear leaked from the corner of her eye…and was wiped by a calloused finger.

Her eyes flew open, and she let out a watery laugh as a familiar purple visage came into view. "I'm not dead," she exclaimed.

"Of course not," he retorted.

She grinned at his matter-of-fact statement. "Well, excuse me for doubting you. The last thing I remembered was passing out."

"A weak female constitution is no excuse for doubting my abilities."

Megan snorted. "I'd like to see you act so tough if you were tied up and beaten."

"Is this another one of your roundabout ways of asking for kinky sex?" He leered at her, and Megan laughed.

It felt good to be alive.

"So how long was I out? And where are we?" she asked, sitting up, and realizing only as the sheet pooled around her waist that she wore not a stitch of clothing.

To his credit—or not—he didn't let his gaze stray to her exposed breasts. "Your injuries required several galactic cycles to mend. As to our location, I've brought us to a secure location so that I can have repairs done to the ship."

"Oops, another delay on my path to auction," she joked, although her heart wasn't truly into it. The thought of being sold didn't irritate her—frighten her yes—but the ache came more from the knowledge that her eventual sale meant she wouldn't enjoy Tren's company—or body—any longer.

"Never fear, you'll get what's coming to you," he announced cryptically, dropping a light kiss on her lips. "Now, are you hungry?"

Megan nodded and watched him saunter out of the room with a spring in his step. She wondered what made him so freaking happy. The knowledge that as soon as the ship got repaired, he could finally get rid of her bothersome ass?

Megan scowled. *Stupid, rotten jerk. He doesn't give a damn that soon I'll belong to someone else.* The realization crushed her. It also destroyed her last wall of denial and forced her to examine the truth of her feelings for him.

Ah, shit. I love him.

How and when had it happened? She didn't like him. He intended to sell her, and yet he roused a passion in her body like no other. He intentionally goaded her until she attacked him, but at the same time, he stimulated her mind and put up with her attitude. Hell, he encouraged it. And she'd fallen hard for him, a useless emotion that now guaranteed he'd break her heart because she didn't suffer under the delusion he felt the same way. Why would he when he could have his pick of women, well, alien females anyway? Why would he want her argumentative, barbaric ass when he could hook up with a docile, dainty bitch?

Megan growled as she thrust the sheets back and swung her legs out of the bed. Standing, she stretched, naked and uncaring. In a mood, she stalked to a brightly lit opening covered with filmy curtains. She stepped through and saw paradise, or something closely resembling it.

Two suns shone in the sky, one much fatter than the other. They made the rolling waves of a large body of water, a sea of the deepest teals, dance and glint with light. Moist, warm air caressed her bare skin. The balcony leaned out over a stone cliff of black rock, but when she looked to the side, she saw a beach stretching in the distance, its white sand sparkling.

She didn't hear Tren join her but felt him at her back, his body brushing up against hers. His arms laced around her torso loosely as he rested his chin on her head.

"How do you like the view?" He asked the question with a lazy casualness she didn't trust.

"It's nice."

"Only nice?" He spun her in his arms, and she peered up at him to see him frowning slightly. "This location is not to your liking? Do you not like warm weather and living along the beach?"

"I love tropical climates. And the place appears gorgeous, but there's not much point in getting too attached." She shrugged. "I mean, this is temporary, right?"

"What if it weren't? Would you mind living long-term in a location such as this?" His gaze bored into hers intently.

She scrunched her nose up at his questions. "What's with the twenty questions?"

"Just curiosity. For the auction, of course. Your new owner will want to know." His lips curved into a smile when he said this, and mirth danced in his eyes.

"You're a jerk," she replied with none of her usual heat. His words depressed her instead of riling her like they usually did.

"I know. Now get your buttocks inside and eat something so I can show you around."

She wanted to ask why he bothered, but he'd already gone through the curtains. Casting a look out over paradise, she could admit—at least to herself— that, if she could have a say in her future, she wouldn't mind a place like this.

Megan went back into the room and saw Tren already lounging on the bed, eating off a laden tray. Hunger of a different sort filled her, and she undulated her hips as she crossed the room toward him. His eyes lit with a glow she recognized, but he didn't move to act upon it. Annoyed, Megan sat cross-legged on the bed to eat, still naked and displaying her pussy, not that he paid her any mind.

She didn't say much as she chewed and watched him as he explained that, other than the staff, they were alone, the guards for his compound housed in a barracks area a short distance away. However, as he continued to elucidate, it didn't mean she shouldn't exercise caution. Megan listened to him and wondered why he bothered with such a long speech extolling the place's virtues. Weren't they leaving as soon as the ship got fixed?

Not that she was that eager to depart. Truthfully, whether she separated from him today or tomorrow, with her heart invested, it would hurt no matter what. So she had a choice: mope about something she couldn't change or enjoy herself while she could.

She'd always hated whiny bitches and refused to turn into one. Once she finished eating, she set the tray aside and crooked a finger at him.

Tren stopped midsentence, and a lusty expression came over his face. "Are you sure? You just woke from a healing sleep. Perhaps you'd like some more fresh air or—"

She sighed. "For a pirate, you're really sucking at the plundering aspect. I mean, what's a captive got to do to get ravaged around here?"

She squealed as he pounced on her, a sound cut short by his lips covering hers in a scorching embrace that stole her breath.

Unlike some of their previous frantic couplings, he took his time with her, caressing her with a gentleness that made her gasp. He explored her mouth thoroughly, his tongue meshing wetly with hers. Megan clung to him tightly, her arms wrapped around his neck, enjoying the feel of his heavier body on hers. He left off her mouth and moved to her neck, licking and nipping at her soft skin. The sharp edge of his teeth scraping at her flesh made her tremble.

"I missed you while you rested in your healing sleep," he whispered as he kissed his way down between her breasts.

"What? You did?" She raised her head to peer down at him incredulously. He gazed back at her, his mien completely serious.

"I did. It's probably a sign of impending mental illness, but I am quite happy you've woken." His lips curved into a crooked smile.

Megan couldn't help her lips from curling into a soft smile of pleasure. "I'm glad you came for me."

"Never doubt me," he growled, his eyes turning dark. He clenched her nipple with his teeth and bit down.

Megan gasped, her body arching under his as his gentle bite sent a jolt straight to her pussy. A chuckle vibrated against her breast before he swirled his tongue around her throbbing tip. Sucking it into his mouth, he sent a never-ending stream of electric zings down to her already damp cleft. He switched breasts, paying equal torturous attention to the other.

When he stopped, she mewled in loss, but he seemed determined to torture her. He moved down her body slowly, his lips caressing her skin softly, driving her crazy with need. He nuzzled the apex of her thighs, and she parted them, her chest heaving as she fought to capture her breath. She lost it in a whoosh as his tongue jabbed at her damp core. Her fingers found his hair and hung on tight as he ate her, his tongue and mouth alternating between nibbling and flicking her clit then delving into her sex. He inserted two fingers into her channel, pumping her with his digits as his tongue skimmed over her sensitive nub. Her pelvic muscles clenched his fingers tight, her hips rocking in cadence to his thrusts.

When he bit her swollen clit gently with the sharp points of his teeth, she bowed off the bed with a scream. He pushed her back down and anchored her with his hands and did it again, applying even more pressure. Her climax crested and crashed with an intensity that made her lose her mind. He grunted with satisfaction as he moved up to cover her body. She shoved at him.

"Get on your back," she ordered. A sensual grin crossed his face as he obeyed, but only to a certain point. As she went to straddle him to return the pleasure, he caught her and flipped her so that her pussy rested above his face. Quivers rocked her pussy as she realized his intention. Sixty-nine was such a lovely number.

His cock, a darker purple than the rest of him, strained from his bare groin, the lack of balls on the outside making it appear even larger. She grasped him at the root, enjoying the way he pulsed in her palm. She laved the pink tip with her tongue, tasting the sweetness of his arousal. She drew him into her mouth with decadent languor. She loved to tease him, to feel her big, brash pirate tremble at her touch. To hear him groan as she sucked his dick, grazing her teeth along its length. But he didn't let her oral torture go unanswered. His hands drew her sex down so that he could probe her with his tongue. Already sensitive from her climax, she quaked and would have moved from the intensity of his touch, but he held her firm, made her a prisoner to his tongue and mouth, rebuilding her bliss.

She tried to ignore what he did to her pussy by bobbing her head up and down the length of him, taking him deep enough to make her throat convulse then out again. He grew in her mouth, his cockhead widening, a signal she'd learned announced his impending climax. Yet again, though, he thought to control their lovemaking. He manhandled her until she faced him again, her throbbing pussy straddling his waist.

Megan smiled at him, lifting herself so that her sex hovered just over the tip of him. His blue eyes flashed with passion. Out shot his hands to grab her around the waist and push her down, ramming his cock up into her. She cried out at the suddenly full sensation, her back arching. She didn't move for a moment, holding him inside of her, enjoying the pulsing strength of him buried in her most intimate part. Leaning forward, she braced her hands on his chest while her hair swung forth to create a private curtain where only she and Tren existed.

Rotating her hips, she ground herself against him, circling and pushing against him in a swirling motion that put direct pressure on her clit and made her moan. His fingers dug into the soft flesh of her hips, his enjoyment spurring her to move harder, faster. He stared at her as they undulated in rhythm, the only sounds the harsh pants of their quickening breath and the soft, wet sound of their joining. She couldn't tear her eyes from his. The intensity in them caught her more firmly than his tractor beam ever had, and she wondered at the change in them. The change in him.

A part of her realized that, since her waking, his attitude towards her had shifted. If she didn't know any better, she'd say he cared for her and no longer hid it. Foolish, hopeful thinking on her part probably, but she couldn't help fantasizing as she leaned down to kiss his lips, bestowing upon him a tender embrace full of the longing and love she felt for him.

As if sensing her fragile emotions, he kept his response just as light and sensual, slowing their pace into a tantalizing tease. A tear at his gentleness escaped and rolled down her cheek. He must have felt it because he stopped all motion.

"You're crying."

"Am not," she retorted, her lie soft and unconvincing.

In a swift motion, he rolled so she lay beneath him. "Open your eyes," he ordered.

She clamped them tight. "No."

"Please."

How could she ignore his plea? She blew out a heavy breath, her throat tight, and opened lids, damp with moisture. His thumb brushed at one eye, smearing the brimming tears.

A spasm crossed his face. "Do you hurt?"

She shook her head. Another lie. She hurt, just not physically like he assumed.

"You are sad?"

She thought about fibbing, but didn't. "A little. Don't worry. I'll get over it."

"Why are you sad?"

She shrugged. "I don't know. I guess I miss home."

His eyes darkened, and his face tightened. "This is now your home."

"Only until you sell me," she snapped back, anger an easier emotion to feel than sorrow.

"And if I were to keep you?" He threw that out there, a word bomb that stole her voice. His brow furrowed. "Why do you not answer? Is the idea so abhorrent?"

He didn't wait for her answer. He kissed her fiercely, possessively. His cock, still buried inside her, began to pump, in and out, quickly thickening and butting against her sensitive inner walls. She clung to him, matching him kiss for kiss, thrust for thrust. She didn't dare speak. Didn't dare hope he meant his words. But she could show him.

They rode the wave to their pleasure together, flesh slapping, breaths tangled, their erotic energy building. He tore his lips from hers as they reached the crest, his eyes blazing with passion.

"You are mine," he growled. With that startling, possessive announcement, he buried his face into the crook of her neck—and bit her.

Megan screamed, not from the pain of him breaking her skin with his sharp teeth, but from the crushing pleasure of her orgasm. Ecstasy rolled over her in a tidal rush, sweeping her up and shaking her with bliss.

And it wouldn't end.

With each suck of her neck, and the blood that surely flowed, the crest of her climax rose higher, and higher. When she thought she would pass out from the potency of it, she discovered paradise. Somehow, Tren touched her soul, a feat she'd never imagined, but how else to explain it? She floated out of her body, which would have been really scary, except Tren found her in that vast, lonely limbo. His own spirit wrapped around hers, twined with it, meshing himself with her in a permanent way that brought with it a sense of completion. Rightness.

Like I've come home.

Chapter Twelve

Tren woke first, and he used that moment to stare in silence at the alien female who'd captured his heart—and soul. Not that he was ready to tell her that yet. He didn't want to give her that much power over him, even if she already unconsciously wielded it.

The stunning realization that he couldn't live without Megan rocked him still. He'd fought an inner battle against caring for her—and lost. His capitulation and admittance when he'd watched over her during her convalescence that he loved her was the driving force behind the reason he'd brought her to his secret hideaway. A first ever.

He'd claimed the planet in his youth and, over the years, had built himself a home and a security system that rivaled that of kings and heads of government. He should know since he'd designed most of theirs.

And he'd brought Megan to it, *brought her home*. He still remained undecided as to what he would do about his acquisitions business. Much of that depended on Megan. His marked mate.

He'd bitten her the night before, unable to stop himself, wanting, actually, make that needing, to claim her. She didn't know it yet, but she belonged to him, forever, whether she liked it or not. He dared hope the former.

As for her belief he still intended to auction her, he kept the ruse up for the entertainment of seeing her get mad. Although he might have to drop it soon because he'd noticed sadness in her eyes the last few times she'd attempted to rile him with it. He couldn't stand to see her upset. Her silent tears during their copulation tore at him and roused a fear in him that she wanted to leave him. *Never!*

He still needed to recover from the anxiety he'd suffered at her capture and beating. *That will never happen again.* He'd hate to be the idiot who ever harmed a hair on her head. If they thought him vicious as a mercenary then watch out because, as a mate, he could promise worse.

Megan stirred against him, and he brushed the hair at her temple back so he could press a kiss there. She sighed softly and wiggled her bottom against him. Blood rushed to his cock, which expanded, but that would have to wait for later. He'd made other plans for the morning.

He whipped the sheet back, and she squealed. "Hey, it's chilly. Give it back."

"Get your lazy human buttocks out of bed, female. We have work to do." She rolled onto her back and shot him a dark look. He grinned in reply, loving how she never let him intimidate her.

"What's with this we? If you have something to do, go ahead. Me, I'm crawling back under the blankets and enjoying this bed some more. After all, someone made sure I didn't get to use it much for sleep last night." She scowled as she said it but couldn't stop the humor from lighting her eyes or the sensual stretch of her body.

Tren's cock jerked in response. Megan smiled as she dragged her hand down over her belly then farther to the curls that crowned her cleft. Tren growled at her teasing maneuver. "Megan," he warned.

"What?" She widened her eyes with mock innocence as she bent her legs and parted her thighs. She'd no sooner exposed her pink flesh than she dipped her own finger into her sex.

Tren was only a male, and a weak one when it came to her it seemed. He fell on her like a ravening beast and gave his mate what she so obviously desired.

Then again, to make sure she could last for the time it took to accomplish his planned task.

After cleansing themselves and feasting on the fruit harvested by his staff from the trees in his personal orchard, he finally managed to get her out into the courtyard where he'd had his rack of weapons hauled out for practice.

She perused them and threw him a questioning look.

"You asked that I teach you self-defense. Welcome to your first lesson," he announced as he stripped his shirt off and flexed his upper body.

Her expression brightened. "Really? I thought you said I didn't need it."

He shrugged. "You don't, because I intend to be all the protection you need, but it was not an unreasonable request in the unlikely event I am not around."

"Aren't you afraid I'll use this knowledge to hurt you?" She smirked as she said this, and Tren laughed.

"You will have to work very hard before you can hope to do that. So come on, my little barbarian. Do your worst."

They spent several units grappling because, as he explained, the first element of defense involved learning what a body was capable of on its own.

She hit the ground often—thankfully he'd padded it ahead of time to protect her more fragile constitution. Each time she landed, she got up and scowled at him with annoyance then cursed him with expressions he'd never imagined. But she didn't complain. She kept picking herself up and rushed him again.

When he called a halt, a sheen of sweat covered her body and her breath came hard.

"Not bad, but I think next time we'll concentrate on a weapon. You're just too tiny to do any real damage," he taunted.

Megan's jaw dropped. "Tiny? Are you kidding me? I've been called a lot of things in my time, but tiny is not one of them. You have seen the size of my ass, right?"

Tren grinned. "I have seen your buttocks and quite enjoy their round softness. Would you care for me to show you how much?"

Megan laughed, and Tren didn't resist approaching her for a passionate kiss. He almost bent her over in the courtyard, so quickly did she fire his passion, but he'd planned another surprise and wouldn't allow himself to become distracted—yet.

Tearing his mouth from hers, he scooped her up into his arms. She laced her arms around his neck as he carried her down the path to the beach.

"Please tell me we're going for a swim?" she asked eagerly.

"If it pleases you. I had the staff bring down some food and a blanket so we might eat outdoors."

"Awesome. A picnic."

Her obvious pleasure made him smile. He'd no sooner set her on the sandy beach than she stripped and ran for the waves, laughing in delight. Tren stood watching her for a moment, his heart swelling uncontrollably tight. A connection existed between them now, invisible yet stronger than any bond he'd ever imagined. He turned his back to unpack the basket, but he could still sense her location and, even odder, catch her emotions. Joy as she caroused in the waves, but, even more awe-inspiring, he could feel her strong affection for him.

He'd never paid attention in the past to the talks of mating among his kind. He'd never expected it to apply to him, although his parents had enjoyed such a bond. The experience far surpassed the bits and pieces he did know.

When he had the blanket arranged to his liking, he joined her in the water, stripping off his clothing first. He sluiced through the waves until he caught her naked body and rubbed it against his. She wrapped her legs around his waist and smiled at him. Her eyes shone, and her lips curved in a smile while her pleasure at his presence wrapped around his being in a warm embrace.

"What are you thinking?" he asked, although he already knew through their bond.

Her grin widened. "About how I'd love to eat something."

"Our repast already awaits us."

She bit her bottom lip and shook her head. "Not for that type of food." She arched one brow at him, and he growled.

"You are insatiable."

"And your problem with that is?"

Tren kissed her in response as he carried her back to the beach and the waiting blanket. He'd just made it to the sand when an alarm went off in the pile of their clothing.

"What is that?" she asked as she let herself slide down his body to stand.

Tren downplayed the alarm. "Probably just a malfunctioning sensor. We'll need to return to the house so I can look into it."

He kept a sharp eye out as they dressed, visually tracking the area all around them. The warning didn't bode well at all, as it indicated a surface breach, which meant someone or something had already penetrated his planetary shield. But no matter, he'd take care of whoever thought to disturb him on his home turf, and he'd do it painfully for having interrupted his tryst with Megan. To be on the safe side, he also keyed in a request for additional support from the barracks, where he'd exiled his usual security guards so he might enjoy some private time with his mate.

Grabbing her hand, he tugged her after him as he pulled out a gun with the other.

"Um, I thought you said it was probably just a bad sensor thing?"

"It always pays to be cautious," he replied as he increased their pace going up the path to the house. She didn't reply, but the bite of her fingers laced in his let him know she understood the gravity of the situation despite his attempt at reducing it.

The very stillness around them bothered him, so he almost sighed in relief when he finally saw motion, scuttling green forms that thought to ambush them. With the house in sight, the path to it clear, Tren pushed Megan forward.

"Quick now. Run inside and hide in the bedroom until I come for you."

She hesitated, and he could see indecision in her eyes. "But what about you? I can't leave you alone."

She worried for him? Tren's chest swelled. "Fear not for me. I can handle this; however, I need you somewhere safe so I am not distracted."

She went on tiptoe to brush his lips before turning to run with a muttered, "You'd better be careful, or I'll hurt you myself."

He grinned at her departing figure, not taking his eyes from her until she'd made it into the house safely. Then his lips curled into a vicious snarl.

Time to take care of the scum who threatened his female.

* * * *

Megan dashed into the house, but she had no intention of hiding and leaving Tren alone to fight. She just wanted to arm herself before she returned to help him. She ran into the main living area but saw nothing of use. What she really needed was something from those racks of weapons she'd seen this morning during her fighting lesson.

She strode into the kitchen, meaning to ask the staff where they'd stashed them, but skidded to a halt. She found the small creatures—who acted as servants and looked like Hollywood's version of green Martians—tied up and gagged.

Which meant some of the bad guys had made it into the house. *Shit.* Megan whirled to run back to the front door and Tren, but hit a brick wall. She tried to back-pedal, but hands gripped her with the strength of iron. She peered up in fright and encountered the familiar leer of Tren's brother.

"Let me go," she yelled.

"No."

She kicked out, hoping to connect, but wise to her previous style of attack, he kept his lower body arched away. She struggled against him, but he reeled her in and slung her over his shoulder. She pounded at his back, shrieking.

"Bully. Tren is going to make you regret this."

"Not before I make him regret what he did to me," Jaro replied with an inappropriate grope.

Megan's blood ran cold as his intent came clear. "Like bloody hell." With no weapon at hand, she remembered what Tren had taught her and used the only weapon she had. She bit Jaro.

He cursed but didn't put her down. "Feisty barbarian. Good thing I came prepared."

A jab in her thigh made her huff in annoyance. "Aw, fuck. Not again. What is it with you aliens and drugging women. Jerrrk." She slurred the last word as the world went fuzzy and she blacked out.

Chapter Thirteen

Tren didn't wait for the encroaching enemy to approach. He charged them with silent fury. A gun in one hand, a knife in the other, he took aim as he went after the invaders. He didn't miss. Nor did he shoot to injure. Each headshot took down an intruder, and those who popped up silently from the rocks and brush met the sharp edge of his blade.

As attacks went, the enemy proved less than impressive. Mindless clones that resembled the slimy skinned goblins of the Pracgudian galaxy, they didn't even wield any laser pistols. Whoever had sent them to attack had armed them instead with knives and swords. To say he sliced through them in a gruesome swath was an understatement. Actually, the ease with which he dispatched them insulted him. *If someone was going to attack me, they could have at least made an effort.*

Unless these fodders for death served another purpose, such as delay. Tren almost groaned aloud at his stupidity in not recognizing the stalling tactic.

Urgency imbued him as, through his connection to Megan, he sensed her sudden shock, then fear. Her anger swiftly followed, but what worried him most of all was when, like a fire snuffed, he no longer felt anything of her emotions.

Tren roared in fury, the icy chill of fear held at bay by the intact tendril of his mating bond allowing him to know she lived, though incapacitated.

Unacceptable.

Tren broke off the battle with the clones and ran toward his house then past it, following his ghostly connection to Megan.

At a swift jog, it didn't take him long to catch up to his brother, who strode along in cocky arrogance with Megan slung over his shoulder.

"Drop her, Jaro, before I put an end to our feud once and for all."

His brother turned with a smirk. "Done with my little surprise already? That must be a record even for you. I'd calculated it would take you at least a few units, enough time for me to get away with the female."

Tren raised his gun and aimed it at his brother's head, his hand steady, even if his heart quavered at what Jaro forced him to do. "Don't make me kill you," he warned.

Jaro scoffed. "You and I both know you won't break our promise to Mother over a female."

Tren felt the coldness of his killer side slip over him. "I will kill anyone who thinks to harm my mate, promise or not."

Jaro's eyes widened, and he reeled back a step. "Mate? Surely you didn't bond with the Earthling? She's a barbarian."

"Megan is my mate. The proof of her claiming is visible on her neck. So I am going to ask you one last time to put her down, or make no mistake, I will kill you."

Before Jaro could comply, a burning pain hit Tren's back. With a growl, Tren turned and fired on the ranks of a new group of aliens approaching armed with laser pistols. A presence at his side made him snarl, a sound bitten short as he saw his brother shooting at the advancing menace.

"Game over, Jaro. Call your lackeys off," Tren shouted.

"They're not mine," Jaro replied, his expression grim as he aimed and fired.

"Frukx!" Tren didn't like the sound of that, but then another worry hit him. *Megan.* He whirled in time to see figures darting toward her prone figure on the ground. Tren roared as he rushed them, shooting them down, but more poured forth from the vegetation as he stood over her body, protecting her unconscious shape with his own.

A few fiery shots struck him, the burning pain making him grit his teeth. It also made him sloppy, and he missed the attack from behind, which toppled him over to lie face first in the ground.

And this is why I became a mercenary instead of a soldier. Sneak attacks are much better for my general health than full-on battle.

The injuries peppering his body would heal if he got to a medtech unit. Tren groaned as he tried to push himself up. He struggled to one knee as the sounds of shouting and renewed firing let him know the guards that he'd sent away during his courtship of Megan had finally arrived from the outpost.

Frantically, he looked about for Megan. When he didn't see her, he staggered to his feet. The sudden movement made him sway, and black spots danced in front of his eyes.

Then he knew nothing.

* * * *

Tren woke in the healing unit, and he bellowed when the frukxn' thing wouldn't let him rise as it completed the mending sequence. His shout brought Jaro, who sported some colorful bruises.

"Where's Megan?" Tren could sense her, faintly. His fragile connection to her frightened him like nothing else ever had.

Jaro's face tightened.

Tren struggled against the invisible bonds that held him while the machine worked and gave up with a frustrated scream of rage. "This is your fault," Tren yelled.

"I'm not the one who kidnapped her," Jaro shouted back.

"But you're the one who frukxed with my security, are you not?"

Jaro at least had the decency to look sheepish. "I only meant to take your human and copulate with her like you did with Shinja. Show you what it felt like to have a female you cared for tainted."

Tren growled. "You idiot! How many times do you have to be told I never touched that she-witch?"

Jaro's lips tightened. "Stop lying. She admitted it to me."

"Because the whore was mad I rebuffed her advances."

"Liar. She loved me, and you just couldn't keep your hands off."

"She was copulating with the whole regiment. I was the only one who said no. Don't believe me? Fine, then call up some of the others from the rank. I'm sure now that all this time has passed, they might finally have the courage to admit their part."

Jaro's face stiffened for a moment then went slack with resignation. "Some already have confessed."

"And?" Tren growled.

"I killed them instead of believing them."

Tren snorted. "They probably deserved it. So are you going to keep believing that good-for-nothing whore or your own brother and common sense?"

"What? And give up our competition for greatest mercenary?" Jaro grinned.

"Ha. What competition? We both know I'm the better one."

"Says the male who had his security system cracked and didn't notice until I intentionally set off an alarm." Jaro smirked in triumph, and Tren scowled.

"I was distracted." And still was with worry about his mate. "How much longer before this blasted thing is done? I need to go after Megan."

"You still have a few units to go, but don't worry, we've almost caught up to the idiot who took her."

Tren laid his head back and closed his eyes in relief. "Good."

"Not really. Z'nistakn is the one who kidnapped her, and he's taking her back to his planet, which is virtually impregnable."

Tren allowed a ghost of a smile to tilt his lips. "No, it's not. I bribed the engineer who designed his system."

"You mean tortured?" Jaro replied wryly.

"Either way, he gave me some backdoor codes to get in."

"How do you know he didn't change them?"

"I killed him right after, of course." Tren chuckled, and Jaro joined him.

"Fine, that gives you a possible way in, but it does nothing to help us with the troops he has on hand to throw at us both on land and in space."

"I'll worry about penetrating his fortress. It is after all my specialty. As for space, I think it's time I called in some favors. I will get her back, Jaro, even if my actions start a war with the entire Galactic Council." Tren couldn't care less about Z'nistakn's position on the council. He'd frukxed with the wrong male when he took their mutual dislike to a personal level.

Jaro sighed. "Great, reunited for not even a galactic unit and already you're dragging me into trouble." He laughed. "Just like the old days."

Tren joined him in chuckling, but his was a darker sound. Where Megan was concerned, he'd do and kill anything to get her back. Woe to anyone who stood in his way.

* * * *

In what rapidly was becoming a tedious pattern, Megan blinked her eyes open, sighed, and kept them open. Not that the view really appealed, but she'd learned playing opossum simply didn't seem to work. Besides, the situation warranted her using her wits because standing in front of her was a cross between an alligator and a human. In other words, something butt ugly. Unlike her other abductions, this time she sat in a chair with only her hands bound in front of her, which left her feet free. What a mistake.

"Finally, she awakes," hissed the creature, flicking out a forked tongue.

She crinkled her nose. "What are you, Voldemort's cousin?"

Slitted yellow eyes narrowed. "Silence female. I am galactic councilor Z'nistakn, but you may call me Master."

A snicker escaped her. "I don't think so. Although I can see calling you my new pair of boots if you don't take me back to Tren, like yesterday." Megan made the threat, even as she didn't hold out hope Tren would rescue her again. Ridiculous as her new captor appeared and spoke, she recognized the signs of wealth from the well-armed guards at his back to the more opulent surroundings around her. Anyhow, it wasn't as if her pirate truly cared for her. He simply enjoyed using her body. It didn't stop her from hoping, though, that he'd come sweeping in, guns blazing to rescue her like Han Solo and Luke had with Princess Leia.

The lizard, whose name she couldn't pronounce, just about went postal at her words. "Insolent whore. I will teach you to mock those superior to you." Its clawed fingers grappled with the robe it wore and spread it open to reveal a stubby penis.

Megan laughed. "Ooh, make me shake in teeny, tiny fear, why don't you? My god, are all your kind so poorly endowed? No wonder you need to kidnap women. Your own probably keep laughing you out of the bedroom."

The titters she heard didn't come from Mr. Lizard, but his guards. And it made him snap. He drew back and slapped her, rocking her head to the side.

Turning back to face him, she smirked. "Lovely, another alien coward who can only hit a woman when she's tied up. Is Tren the only alien in the galaxy man enough to handle a real woman?" She really should learn to shut up, she thought, as Mr. Lizard smacked her again and again, but honestly, she'd rather die than let the alligator freak touch her.

A beeping sounded, and a computer-generated voice announced, "Request for teleconference from Trenkaluan for galactic councilor Z'nistakn."

The upright crocodile stopped slapping her, and his slitted eyes lit with pleasure. "About time. I was beginning to wonder if my troops had killed him during your extraction."

Megan's heart almost stopped at those words. *Was Tren hurt? Oh, my god.*

The lizard turned away from her and faced a large blank wall. "Put him onscreen."

Tren's face filled the wall, his blue eyes almost opaque in his fury. "Z'nistakn," he snarled. "You've crossed the line."

The alien crowed. "Ah, has the mighty mercenary suffered a loss? So much for your reputation of always prevailing."

Mercenary? Megan's brow furrowed. Tren was a space pirate, or was he? Suddenly some of the things he'd said and done came together, and she wanted to laugh at her naivety. Mercenary or not, she still loved the stupid, purple lug.

"You will return Megan to me this instant or suffer the consequences," Tren ordered.

"I think not. Well, not until you've done a few tasks for me. Then we can talk about a possible exchange."

"You sign your death warrant then."

"It will take more than threats to frighten me," scoffed the lizard.

Tren's lips curled into a sadistic smile that made her shiver, not in fear for herself, but in satisfaction. The idiot who'd kidnapped her didn't seem to realize he played with fire. "That wasn't a threat. It was a promise."

The alien laughed. "You seem to forget I have an army at my disposal. Actually, as we speak, I've already dispatched my squadrons to take care of your vessel if you refuse to cooperate."

Tren's smile widened. "Who says I came alone?" The view on the screen switched to show one tiny ship hovering in space, and then suddenly, there were dozens of vessels of varying sizes.

A stink permeated the room as Mr. Lizard almost shit himself in sudden fear. His voice quavered when he spoke again. "You wouldn't dare! The council won't sit back and allow you to kill me. It would mean a declaration of war against your kind if you did."

Tren's eyes narrowed, becoming flat and cold. Megan could almost feel the chill creeping from them. "If it takes a war to get my mate back, then bring it on. I am coming for her. And when I do, you and anyone else in my way will die."

The communication cut off, and the scaly alien went into panic mode, screeching orders.

Megan, however, couldn't lift her jaw up off the ground.

Mate? Did he just refer to me as his mate? A grin spread across her face. He'd not only come for her, but he loved her enough to start a galactic war. How cool was that? *Nothing says I love you like bloodshed and violence.*

Nearby explosions sent vibrations through the room, and Megan jumped up from the chair and moved to put her back against a wall just as the lizard turned to face her.

"You! Come here, female. Since you mean so much to him, then I'll need you to escape. He won't dare harm me if you're in my possession."

"If you want me, come and get me," she taunted. The lizard advanced on her just as the door to the room blew open. Megan, though, didn't dare let her eyes stray from the advancing alien, even as the wails of dying creatures filled the air. Along with the screams came the acrid smell of burning flesh and plastic, which made her nose twitch and her eyes water.

A roar of pure fury swept through the room, but Megan didn't have time to grin or look as her purple marauder arrived to the rescue. The lizard freak reached her and made to grab her. Megan dodged the claws and pumped her foot up hard. With a squeal of pain, the lizard bent over double. Then he went sailing across the room as Tren arrived and tossed him aside like rubbish.

A second later, he crushed her to his chest— one armed because the other hand was still busy firing. He planted a quick bruising kiss on her lips and then tucked her behind him. A gun in each hand, he picked off the remaining troops until the only groaning body left belonged to Mr. Lizard.

Tren holstered one pistol before tucking her under his arm, tight against him. "Are you injured?" he asked gruffly.

"Just a few bruises. You got here just in time."

"I would have arrived sooner, but Jaro forced me to wait for backup." His disgruntled tone warmed Megan as they strode over to the councilor, who tried to crawl away. Tren planted a black boot on his back and flattened him.

"I'm glad he made you wait; otherwise, your chance of succeeding would have ended up a lot slimmer. Besides, what matters is you came to save me in the first place."

Almost opaque blue eyes swiveled to meet hers. "I will *always* come for you." He turned away as he pointed his gun at the lizard's head.

Megan grabbed his arm. "Wait. Should you do that? What if it starts a war with your people?"

Tren fired, and the alien's head disappeared in a splatter of things best left unmentioned. "Your safety is worth more than any blood or mayhem that emerges from my actions this day."

Megan gaped up at him. "Are you saying what I think you're saying?"

Tren turned and shot over her head at something that squealed. "Can this conversation not wait until we've made it back to safety?"

"Oh, fine. Change the subject. Isn't that just like you?" she ranted. "Here, do something useful then since you won't admit the obvious." She held up her bound hands. Tren yanked a knife from a sheath and sliced through the restraints. Freed, Megan stooped and grabbed a gun.

"What are you doing?" he barked.

"Helping of course," she replied.

"You can help by staying out of the way."

Megan grinned. "Make me."

Upended over his shoulder, her breath left her in a whoosh. She watched the play of the muscles in his buttocks as he carried her to safety. And to make sure he hurried, she stroked them.

Chapter Fourteen

Tren didn't relax until they'd made it back to his ship, a return trip made much easier by the fact that most of Z'nistakn's troops disappeared when they sighted him; their courage had flown with their leader's life. A good thing, too, considering the distraction hanging over his shoulder. His naughty mate, instead of succumbing to hysterics, toyed with him, urging him to hurry because as she stated emphatically, "I'm dirty and horny."

He quickened his pace and, upon boarding his craft, which he'd landed even before the battle and ultimatum, headed straight for his quarters.

Jaro waylaid him on his way to his chambers, standing in front of him like an immovable wall. Tren almost shot him, his patience wearing thin. "Get out of my way," he growled.

"The Galactic Council's been calling."

"Tell them I'm busy," Tren barked, the throbbing need in his loins more important.

Jaro smirked. "I think having a mate has addled your brains, a fate I hope to never suffer. But mental problems aside, before you go bury yourself in her, you should know that there will be no reprisals for our actions today. On the contrary, Z'nistakn recently earned a removal order which, since we took care of it, will mean a nice credit boost to us both."

Tren didn't bother arguing about the split in the profit, even though he had been the one to kill the slimy councilor. "Fine. You've given me your news. Now move."

Jaro held up a hand. "Hold on, there's more. With the recent opening of a seat on the council, and given your loyal work, they've nominated you to the position. A great honor for our people, as you know."

"Tell them no. I don't do politics." Too cutthroat, even for him.

"He won't have time," piped in Megan. "Because he'll have his hands full with me."

"Silence, female." Tren smacked her bottom, not hard, but she squeaked anyway and pinched his buttocks in retaliation. Tren almost took her right against the wall, brother watching or not. He restrained himself—barely.

Jaro shook his head. "Refuse that kind of honor? You can tell them then. I'm just playing messenger."

"Now go play bridge commander and don't bother me unless something needs killing," Tren ordered. Jaro laughed as he stepped aside finally.

Tren stalked past him and slapped the console leading into his room. He slid the portal shut, cutting off his brother's laughter.

Striding right into the ablutions chamber, Megan still over his shoulder, he didn't bother removing their filthy garments as he stepped right into the cleansing stall. A press of a button and the lasers began their cleansing, disintegrating their clothing, which proved interesting as it placed the tempting flesh of Megan's bare buttock in the perfect position for nibbling.

He didn't resist, and she squealed. "Are you going to put me down?"

It took another bite before he answered. "What if I don't want to?"

"Then you're going to find fucking me a bit of a challenge," she retorted.

Tren couldn't stop the grin at her saucy remark. Even though Megan found herself kidnapped and slapped around, nothing could quell her indomitable spirit. He allowed her to slide down his body, slowly, the smooth friction of her skin against his firing his blood to a boiling point. Fragments of their clothing remained caught between their bodies, so he turned her, allowing the particle cleanser to remove them.

Whirling her back around, he caught sight of the bruises marring her visage. He stroked a finger gently down the curve of her cheek. "I'm sorry. This should never have happened. We should get you to the medtech unit."

Megan caught his hand and placed a kiss in the palm. "I'm fine. I'd rather show you how happy I am that you came for me."

"You are mine, Megan, even if you are a smart-mouthed barbarian." He tempered his words with a smile.

"If this is your way of saying you love me, then ditto, my freakishly large, purple pirate. Or should I say mercenary?" She arched a brow at him, and he grinned sheepishly.

"Retired mercenary turned acquisitions specialist. And now your mate."

"Mate, huh? And what does being your mate mean?"

Tren hoisted her up by the waist and placed her back against the wall. "It means," he replied, thrusting his cock into the moist channel that welcomed him, "that you belong to me, and I belong to you." Her legs wrapped around him as she watched him with bright eyes. "It means, if someone kidnaps you, I will come to your aid and kill them, violently and painfully." Her slick channel squeezed around him. "It means that even if you drive me insane with your chatter and try to maim me, I will punish you with exquisite pleasure until you scream my name in climax." Digging his fingers into her buttocks, he bounced her on his shaft, the molten, snug feel of her sex driving him wild. "It means I will love and cherish you forever, no matter what."

"Oh, Tren. I love you so much." She didn't say anything more, unless he counted the shrill scream as she orgasmed around his cock. The tight grip of her milking pelvic muscles brought his own bliss, and he jetted into her with a yell.

Chests heaving, they clung to each other, and Tren smiled.

It might have taken him traversing to the far ends of the galaxy and accidentally abducting a barbarian female to find love, but he'd do it and a lot more all over again if it meant he got to keep Megan as his mate—forever.

Epilogue

Several galactic cycles later…

Megan wandered into the command center of the starship and found Tren sitting in his chair, grinning. She draped herself on his lap, her arms going around his neck to draw him close for a kiss. He obliged with a quick peck that made her frown, especially since he seemed about to burst with glee.

"What's got you in such a good mood?" she asked. In other words, what distracted him so much that he hadn't yet thrown her down to ravish her?

"I got you a present." He swiveled her to face forward on his lap, and she heard him tap the console. The wall screen lit up with a view she recognized.

She made a moue of distaste. "Earth? You brought me home. But why? I've already got everything I need."

"Everything except for one crucial thing," he replied mysteriously. A keystroke later and the screen changed to the cargo bay. The camera zoomed into a cage, and Megan's breath whooshed out.

"You caught Cameron for me?" The jerk who had tried to kill her so long ago and launched her on the adventure of a lifetime. Her ex-boyfriend sobbed in his cage, and Megan shook her head at his craven behavior. *And to think I once slept with that.* Thank god she'd acquired better taste. *Once you go purple, baby, you can never go back.*

"Initially, I'd planned to string him by his heels, rip open his stomach, and feed him his own entrails, but while excruciating, it would have ended too quickly. And I want him to suffer for what he did to you."

Twisting on his lap, she squirmed until she looked into his pure blue eyes, now hard and cold like ice. "Well, you know, he did start the chain of events that brought me to you."

"Which is why I'm not planning on torturing him eternally. However, he needs to pay for what he did to you."

Her lips curled at the wicked look on his face. "You have a plan, don't you?"

Tren didn't immediately answer as he shifted her legs to straddle him. "I know a brothel that deals in more perverted sexual acts, and they're looking for a male screamer."

Megan laughed. The old her might have been a little appalled at what Tren intended to do to Cameron. The new her, forged in love and adapting to a new, more violent reality, grinned. "Oh my god, that is so deliciously evil."

"I was hoping you'd like it."

"Like it? I love it. Not as much as I love you, though, my purple pirate."

"Mercenary," he growled.

Megan smirked. They kept having this argument—on purpose, of course. She squealed when he stood and upended her over his shoulder.

"That's it, back to bed you go until you learn your lesson."

"And which one would that be?" she sassed.

"I am a mercenary, the most feared one in the known universe, and you will obey me or suffer the consequences."

"I'd rather you be my pirate and ravish me."

He smacked her ass and then rubbed his hand against the crease of her cleft. "You are never going to let me forget I accidentally abducted you, are you?"

"Nope. But don't worry, I still love you."

"And I love you, my beautiful, feisty barbarian. But don't tell anyone, or I'll have to kill them."

Her laughter rang out, filled with all the joy she'd discovered in her alien lover's arms.

In the end he made love to her, and while they still argued about his title, he taught her that she should always speak her mind. The results were just too pleasurable not to.

* * * *

Meanwhile, in a galaxy, far, far away…

Jaro woke and shook his head in confusion. He blinked, and then blinked again at what he saw, none of which made sense. The last thing he recalled, his ship had been hit by some kind of electromagnetic pulse and he'd lost all control of his craft.

Apparently, though, he'd survived, even if his situation appeared odd considering he found himself spread-eagle on a soft surface. Pulling at his arms and legs, he scowled as he discovered them restrained. Craning his head, he also noticed that he appeared to have lost his clothing.

Then again, so had the female who entered his field of vision. Pale of skin like the barbarian female his brother had mated with, the petite beauty possessed a pair of full breasts with pink tips pierced with golden rings. Her hair, a fiery red curtain, fell past her waist and matched that of her pubes. Green eyes flecked with gold regarded him with cool interest.

Despite his situation, Jaro couldn't help the surge of lust that made his cock rise. She didn't miss it either, and she trailed her gaze over his body, her look heating his blood and expanding his prick even farther.

Her nipples tightened, and her lips pursed as she approached him. She ran a finger, edged with a sharp nail, down his chest. Jaro's body trembled, consumed with a desire to claim this female, to thrust into her tight body and devour her luscious breasts until she came, clawing at his back.

A firm grip wrapped around his shaft, and he sucked in a breath, unable to stop himself from arching his hips up. Slowly, she stroked him, and the smell of her arousal filled the air, a decadent aroma that drove Jaro wild with lust.

"Untie me," he said hoarsely, eager to give her what she plainly desired.

The motion on his cock halted, and her eyes stopped their perusal of his body. Her gaze flicked up to meet his, and caught him. "I don't think so, purple warrior. I have need of your body, and this position suits me just fine."

Jaro frowned. "I don't understand."

She clambered onto the bed and straddled his waist, her moist core hovering over the tip of his prick. "You will soon. Don't worry. I won't hurt you—much."

The End but for more purple mercenary adventure check out EveLanglais.com

Printed in Great Britain
by Amazon